The Fragments that Remain

I am not a writer. I am the Painter Twin. Ally is the Writer Twin. Despite the fact that we were each given different materials at a young age, Ally continues to pester me to try writing, so here I am with paper and pen.

What turns me away from writing is that I am never sure what to write about. Painting is easier. I can watch nature documentaries and do abstracts of the animals or blend different colors on the canvas with objects or people in the foreground. But writing? My worst grade is in English.

I asked Ally what I should write about if he wants me to do it so badly. He said to write about something that makes you happy and something that makes you sad, so here I am writing about this morning.

MaamaaBaabaa left us in charge of the bookshop. We have been encouraging them to do the weekend yard sale book hunting together for years. It would be good for them to have time away from the kids, we said, but really, it would give us time to be parent-free.

With instructions for one of us to run the register and the other to sweep and dust around the mountains of bookshelves, they left us behind for the first time. We are fifteen and yet we did the celebratory dance we have been doing since we both could walk as soon as they were out of eyesight.

First things first: we turned off the old radio and turned on the portable speaker we pooled our money for last summer. Ally's braids were swaying as he danced to the rezzy rap filling the shop. Second part of the plan: our mutual childhood best friend, Krish, breezed in the door and immediately tried rapping along to the lyrics.

A perfect morning.

The best part is the control of the music. Usually, if the speaker is brought into the shop, it is because Maamaa wants her Elvis of the North playing. Upstairs, the four of us (sometimes five if Krish is there) will dance and sing along to the alternating First Nations hip-hop and electric powwow music as a regular family activity. Baabaa thinks it is not appropriate to play our music in a small business (the customers that have come in so far haven't complained) and insists we play the local rock station on the radio. MaamaaBaabaa are not here and we are proving them wrong.

The second best part is the atmosphere. We are kids playing at being adults in the shop we will one day run together, the morning sunlight casting shadows behind bookshelves and exposing the dust Ally sends into the air. I am laughing and singing along with my favorite people in the world. It is a time of laughter and teasing and existing freely.

We do not have a reserve to go home to during hunting season, we do not have a *Nokomis* to make us bannock (Baabaa does that instead), we do not have relatives dragging us on the summer powwow trail. What we do have is music written by descendants of Turtle Island. For now it is enough but both Ally and I have talked about wanting more.

This yearning hits hard when Krish's Maa comes to get him for lunch. She has always treated us as her own as our family has done for Krish and we welcome Auntie Komal when she enters the shop. She says good morning and carries the delicious aromas from her restaurant next door as she searches for her son in the bookshelves. I know from the cash register when she has found him because they immediately begin to speak in their language.

Ally and I have grown up listening to the rhythms of the fast-paced conversations in their households and it feels like home to hear it. At the same time, it pushes a hole into my chest. I would give anything to be able to converse in our ancestral language. I know colors and some animals and a few kitchen terms from our Native Second Language classes in elementary and grade nine but I can't hold a conversation.

It turns my perfect morning sad and I turn off our music despite Ally's protests.

Part I

You had always said that I was too quiet; that I stayed hidden in a shell safe away from the world. That there was so much hidden inside, if only I would crack the glass it was held within.

How could I break the glass?

Why was I so afraid?

You decided I needed to write, no I needed a life, no I needed friendship, no I needed religion, no I needed social skills, no I needed to be filled with burning desire, no I needed to simply learn how to live.

So critical, never content.

You said I never lived to my full potential. You believed you lived at peak potential with your overfilled notebooks covered in scribblings, with your booming laughter and lopsided grin.

And how well did that work out for you?

We were mirror images on the outside. The same shape of a face, painted from the same palette, the similar shine within, so capable of many remarkable things, so capable of touching others. We could have been identical twins.

We had vastly different insides.

You were burning, a light so bright that you could captivate a room. I was a warm glow, the rising sun, loved but nothing new.

Polar opposites, they called us.

You were born late, in the time of new beginnings and hope for what was to come. I was born early, in the darkest part of the year, in the time of enjoying the silence and basking in candlelight. Everyone was drawn to you, never able to get enough of your essence. I stood on the sidelines, comfortable away from the gaze of others.

Honorary twins, they called us. Partners in crime from the moment I opened my eyes and saw the exact same pair staring back.

I relish in the memories of slipping out of the shop into the streets to look at the city lights during the long nights. *Here comes double trouble,* they would say with floating laughter as we barreled around the aisles, dodging the customers and the stacks upon the floors.

How can the duo continue when only one is left standing?

We were supposed to walk down that long aisle together. Hundreds of eyes on us, most would not have known us. Just a pair of twins strutting down the rubber mat like they owned the place. A procession of accomplishment, ready to receive awards and to be handed blank rolled papers because diplomas were not allowed to be rolled and therefore must be mailed.

You were not there.

We were supposed to eat with Krish after, fill up on his family's delicious foods that were responsible for you being a chubby child. Perhaps find a party to crash, a city full of graduating teens? There were numerous parties on every street.

You were not there.

The pairs were chosen ahead of time, taken from the perfect even number of our graduating class. Administration should have known better than to believe everyone would graduate.

I pulled the short stick after all that happened and walked that aisle alone. I did not want to do it at all, but Maamaa convinced me to walk for graduation. Raved about wanting to see *one* of her children down that aisle. Told me to smile for the pictures.

"Do not dwell on the dead, *daanis.* We must celebrate their life as well as our own," Baabaa advised, his heavy hand on my shoulder.

"He would have wanted you to celebrate your graduation," Krish said, his quick hands weaving my braids.

Would you have wanted your little twin walking down the aisle alone? A spectacle that screams I AM AN ONLY CHILD NOW.

You forced me to walk with you. Could not understand why your little mirror pushed herself on the floor instead of running alongside you. I was dragged along, your hand pulling me up when I began to fall. *I will keep you up, Andy.*

I rewatched the home videotapes over and over so many times I am surprised they did not crack. A smiling baby, so excited to be in a big brother's shadow and at his side constantly. Tripping along in your hand-me-down overalls, too-large shirts fashioned into dresses, never bothering with shoes because they were never in your possession. An excited preschooler, repeating affirmations and encouragements like they were a mantra. *Very good! Five more steps! Head up, shoulders back!* I loved your attention, loved your unconditional love.

You wanted me to do everything you could do; how could I refuse?

We were supposed to walk down every aisle together. Kindergarten. Elementary. Flashes of impish grins spreading across spotted faces. High school, college, perhaps university. We would have grown into our grins by then, our faces no longer rounded with childhood. We even had plans to walk each other down the wedding aisle (Baabaa would officiate). It was only fitting that our other half from the beginning of our lives would escort us to the other half for the rest of our lives. We were awaiting a life in which we would be separated. No longer greeting the morning together, no longer side by side as often as possible. Until those days came upon us, we were to be inseparable. Never apart unless absolutely necessary. Holding each other tall against the world.

You keep me up, I keep you up, remember?

I suppose you didn't.

There were twelve months of your existence that I was not there.

You would argue that no, it was four months that I was not there. You believed that our spirits attached to the bodies when the heart was formed. That the moment a beating organ began to build, the *gitchi-manitoo* sent a sliver of the invisible to the developing body. This was not the case for every fetus, in your mind. No, only the ones meant to be alive were gifted by the invisible.

You swore on everything you held dear that your first memory was of being in Maamaa's arms and feeling a connection with the raspberry hidden in the nest of her hips. Maamaa recounts of you knowing before she did. Always clinging to her lap and laying your head against the spot that would become my first home. She was not surprised when two lines showed on the stick. *Before ten months you are divided between the dead and the living. Very attentive to spirits,* she would say.

You were always in my life. The first and last face I saw in the sunlight. Our spirits tethered to each other in a way that no one could explain. We could pick up on each other's emotions, exactly how the other was feeling. We insisted we were twins. *Being born in the same year means twins,* we always said. Forget the conception dates and the birth months.

At some point in our lives, that emotional satellite broke. No longer could I tell exactly where you were in the city. No longer could I pick up on your drop in emotions. I thought that maybe we were just growing up, starting to separate from our codependence. I soon came to realize that it had something to do with your newfound grins.

Do you know that I felt when the last of our connection was severed? I felt the shears that cut away our threads. I knew you were gone. We were supposed to die together. If I had been home, would you have lived?

The new year came, and it was the first year of my life without you.

It is always said that the first few days, weeks, months are the hardest. That eventually it will get better, that you will find a new way of living without your now-deceased loved one. I think the people that say that have the same ideals as Maamaa.

I woke up when the threads were cut. A pain so excruciating I felt like I was dying along with you. I ran out the door before he even stirred. It didn't take long to get to the shop: creeping down their fire escape, a few running strides on the street, into the shop and up the entrance to our apartment behind the counter. It was not easy coming home the next morning from Krish's and finding a crime scene in your bedroom.

Baabaa opened the door before I could burst in, and he held me against the wall to keep me from seeing it. I hated him at that moment. Could he not sense that I needed to be in our room at that moment? Baabaa is young for a man of his age and yet he could not hold back the fury that I had become at that moment. I saw your face before they covered it up. It still haunts my eyelids.

Going back to school was difficult but not the hardest part. I would have wanted to hide in the shop forever and become one with the broken bookshelf I made my nest. Alas, I was a senior, and if I wanted to graduate, I needed to go back. I had no intentions of finishing in the summer like Baabaa wanted me to. People stared. Rumors were created, and when one of the twins that were never seen apart is permanently separate, people stare. Krish took care of me. Never leaving my side and appointing his cousins in my classes to sit next to me. After a while, the spotlight left me, and everyone forgot.

I developed a new routine, told Maamaa I was going to the meetings, stayed busy, and stayed focused. I want to tell you that I wallowed in sadness and could never get up in the morning but that is not me. I plowed through the pain and did what I needed to do in order to keep my head above water.

Sometimes I wonder when my hardest part will come.

That does not mean that this is not hard. I won't let them take your things. I am not *coping* the way I should. I should relinquish your earthly things and focus on life. Maamaa says I need to move on. She thinks that because I do not want to empty our room of your things that I am not moving on. That I cannot focus on the promises we made to each other before your death.

Death is the only promise in life, don't you know? We are born one day, and we will all die one day. We were raised in Maamaa's philosophy that death is not a sad thing.

Life is suffering and life is love but death is the end of it all. It is the release of worldly things. The hopes for a new adventure. If you are upset over a death, you are really upset for egoistic reasons.

As per Maamaa's beliefs, we held a celebration of life. Not a wake in a cold stuffy room that smells of rot and formaldehyde. Our family bookshop and Krish's family restaurant closed down for business but kept the doors open. Krish and his parents spent all day cooking a feast and all those that knew you floated in and out to pay respects and celebrate your almost eighteen years. It was kind of a New Year's party in a way. I think you would have liked it.

Maamaa is wrong.

I cannot let you go. I cannot move your things out of our room. I never wanted my own room.

I want my brother.

No amount of celebrating and philosophy will change that.

We received our college offers the month after you died. I didn't apply to more than the college, but you applied everywhere you could. You said you wanted to explore our province and possibly the country as fast as possible. At the time, I was envious of your adventurous attitude. It was nice to daydream about running off to some faraway university, even if I was too scared to apply anywhere. In truth, I had no plans to continue my schooling at all when I could just work at the shop.

I start this week. Well, really it starts next week but the college has a week of orientation activities to make the first years and international students feel comfortable on campus.

I am not staying on campus when I can stay at home for free. Maybe I should have applied for a dorm — it would get me away from our room.

I wish Baabaa wasn't making me go. I'd rather stay home and work at the shop in my free time. It was the exact same discussion we had about me attending school in general. I wanted to start working immediately, but they think it's better I have a diploma in something other than high school.

As for the orientation week, Baabaa says it will help me make friends. I don't see why I need to make friends. I have friends. Well, Krish is already living at his uncle's down south for school, but that doesn't mean I don't have friends.

Okay, maybe he is right.

Maamaa says I need to stop being a pessimist. *You attract the energies you give out*, she has been saying to me a lot.

I can tell Maamaa is disappointed in how hard I have been taking this. Really, I don't think I'm doing so bad. I never went catatonic. I kept moving, focused on finishing senior year. Focused on trying not to let the nightmares get to me.

She wanted me to see counseling when they first took you away, said I would benefit from grief counseling, but I don't like the idea of someone economically benefiting from my pain. I have a handle on this. Probably better than if our roles were reversed; you always were the more expressive of us.

You would've taken the counseling; most likely they would have encouraged you to focus on your writing. I don't have an outlet where I can write out my feelings.

Maybe that's why I've started writing to you.

Dear Brother,

I suppose if what I am truly doing is writing to you, I should start addressing a letter or two. So here I am, forcing my hand to trace the invisible letters in the air no matter how much I shake.

Dear Brother, I miss you.

Dear Brother, I am without you, and I feel as if I am with you in the realm of absence. A broken spirit writing to a spirit that cannot read anymore. A spirit that may not even exist anymore.

Dear Brother,

The first time I wrote, it was over March break. Krish went to visit his cousins as usual, and I was alone. Usually, I had a handle on your death. Even a few months after. And then suddenly I didn't.

The walls had started closing in. Without the stimulation of Krish and his family, I was left to my own devices. Baabaa kept telling me to stop working so much and freaking out the customers by talking to them too much. Of course, I didn't listen and stopped updating my time sheet if I went over my allotted hours.

Studying also became a focus. It was easier to focus on deadlines and coursework than the locked room in the apartment.

I tried to meticulously stay as occupied as possible, but the smallest amount of time without stimulation started to wear on me fast. I started seeing your face when I closed my eyes while conscious. It was easier to force my body to go rigid and stop breathing than it was to go into hysterics. Basically, I have been spending the last several months steeling myself against emotion. It's not sustainable.

So, I began to write.

Dearest Departed,

I do not know when I decided I was going to write. I am not a writer. You are.

You *were.*

It was another gut-wrenching night, sleep embracing everyone but me. I wove between the shelves, straightening books that weren't crooked. I had since taken on the habit of moving my mouth, forming words that could not be heard by the living.

I felt like a fraction of myself, but I was also never myself to begin with.

Pace the shelves, avoid the reflection in the windows and door, leave the lights off. My feet began to ache, but at least I was able to feel something more than the grown emptiness.

Perhaps it was because I was reorganizing the front desk for another countless time, or perhaps I felt your spirit calling through my own. Suddenly a crumpled paper from the discard bin was being flattened and the dying pens were being used until I could breathe again.

Dear Ally,

When I am able to sleep, I dream of you and our memories. For a few hours I am not suffocated by reality and relive the blissful times.

It first started in the shop. It was a slow day and I lost track of how many hours it was since I could last close my eyes without seeing your face. The fatigue wrapped around me in a heavy wool blanket like the dusty one on the couch and I fell asleep at the counter.

The memory was simple: We wanted to be big kids that didn't need Velcro shoes anymore because we were freshly graduated from kindergarten. With Krish, we gathered every pair of shoes in both households. We filled Maamaa's biggest suitcase (the one Krish and I sent you down the stairs in) with all the shoes and, as three, lugged it up the stairs and into the living room. The suitcase was dumped out around the paper copies Mr. Monroe had given us on the last day of school on how to tie shoes.

That day was filled with giggles and lighthearted frustration, interrupted when Auntie Komal brought over tiffin and continued until every shoe was knotted past recognition. Every morning we woke up and the laces were untied, ready for another day of practicing. This continued for three weeks until we left the shoes properly tied and celebrated with a night that included a special trip to the movie rental store down the street and sleeping in a pillow fort.

In late August we started grade one and taught everyone how to tie their shoes. It wasn't as fun as the days we spent practicing but it made us all feel good and our new teacher gave us extra stickers.

Dear Brother,

I am dreading leaving the cozy confines of the building. I feel almost alive when I am here. If I go outside will the sun burn me? Will I join you?

I get into such fits that I swear I need a good smack. I am forever pestering Baabaa, asking if I should bring an umbrella because the forecast is clear, but it might not always be, or if I should bring rubber boots or a parka.

It is times like that when I feel ashamed. He already lost his son and now he is losing his daughter to her own swallowing emptiness.

Dear Ally,

Maamaa dragged me outside. Told me to start walking to the dumpster instead of tossing the bags. If you remember, my aim despite my long legs made the gym teachers sad, and all it does is annoy our mother.

The idea of fresh air felt more suffocating than our room and she had to pull her towering child out onto the pavement. I wanted to fight like a toddler. I wanted to fight as hard as you did against eating peas. Alas I feel as much an embarrassment already; I saw no reason to make her feel worse. I figured that she would force me to stand there for a few seconds and then let me run back inside.

As usual, that is not our mother. She pulled me out and went back inside, knowing the door automatically locked and that there was no way for me to get back in unless I walked away from the door and made my way outside of the back-alley way to the street.

Baabaa eventually took pity on me and opened the door, barely looking at me as I ran in faster than a cat jumps out of a filled tub.

She wasn't being the nicest, but I wouldn't be the nicest to myself either if I was in her position.

Dear Ally,

As usual, Baabaa was smarter than me.

It was a fun week of activities. The first day we had to match up for one of those three-legged races. I teamed up with a girl who was (surprisingly) taller than me. Safe to say we fell more than we could run but I think I made a friend.

Her name is Delilah and she's not from the region. She lives off campus like I do but she doesn't live with her parents. She made that very clear when we first introduced ourselves.

It was a relief to interact with someone who has no prior knowledge of you. I have the opportunity to be my own person for the first time. An only child.

We partnered up for the rest of the week and made plans to see each other out of school. We really clicked after our race. She has a calming presence that makes me feel better than I have in months. She is really interested in the shop, and I promised to bring her one day. Maybe I will even tell her about you one day.

I had to cut the last letter short — Delilah called and invited me over. MaamaaBaabaa were beaming when I said I was going to a friend's house. They insisted I bring food. I insisted that I could take the bus.

She has a roommate; his name is James. He is so energetic. He cannot stop talking unless you tell him to be quiet. It reminds me a lot of you before you tested how much your insides could take; after that you got louder.

Delilah is the opposite.

The moment I walked into the apartment I felt the serenity of her space. I feel so drawn to her it frightens me a little, but I think it is just because her essence helps calm my mind. She is so calming that I did not want to leave at the end of the night.

She is an oil spill on fire. Beautiful in a way that you know you should stay away from. Her skin glistens in the sun the same way oil does. Maybe I am imagining the rainbows. If it were not for the incredibly tall and lanky girl that picked me out of the crowd, I would have secluded myself even more.

It is so easy to be around them. Much easier than it is with Krish's cousins (although I am grateful for them). The moment I stepped into their apartment, it was as if I got a fresh set of lungs. It was the first time I had gone over two hours without seeing black spots from lack of oxygen. The atmosphere in the living space was similar to the feeling Delilah gives off. Welcoming and wholesome. The hours slipped away faster than I thought, and I found myself sad about going home.

Dear Brother,

Having my own friends is easier than I thought it would be. I'm so used to sharing everything that I feel greedy having my own friend group. The thing that makes me feel the guiltiest is that the best part about it all is that they only know me.

They find *me* interesting, they love the idea of the shop, and we get to know each other more and more each day. They're both so open and intrigued by anything. It's a little scary but I also like it.

They've shown me a few shows they've been meaning to watch and it's the framework for our weekly hangouts. We help each other with classes if we need it. Delilah is always cooking something new, and we make a big event of it.

I can see myself spending my adulthood with them. Weekly binge watches with home-cooked meals. Genuine friendships that could last a lifetime. I'm so glad Delilah chose me for the three-legged race.

Dear Brother, you would be glad

I have quickly developed a new routine. I attend class, complete coursework on campus, go home to work in the evenings or spend time with my friends. We make plans to do other things outside their apartment as well. Yesterday we went to the art museum with another one of Delilah's friends. Her name is Helena.

I have never had a friend group to call my own. We have always shared friends and for the longest time it was just us and Krish. Now, I have people that have never even heard of you. I've said it before, but as bad as it is to admit, I like it this way. I am no longer in your shadow. No longer am I seen as *Ally's little sister*. Now, I am simply Andy.

To these people, I am able to be whoever I want to be.

The truth is, I have no clue who I am without you. I am hoping they will be able to help guide me into becoming my own person. I will have to tell them one day in order for that to happen, but I am building myself up to that.

Dear Brother,

I have gone over the future conversation multiple times in my head. Most of the time I expect that it will have to come up in passing. Just a simple *my brother and I used to do that all the time as kids* or *I can't sleep on my own, I've never had my own bedroom* or the even more cryptic *my brother died the same way.*

Basically, I don't want to talk about it at all.

I like my little bubble of friends left untainted by the emptiness in my chest that grew when they found you. It's one thing to have regular discussions about our mental health to check in with each other but it is completely different to tell them my secret.

And it feels like a secret.

You are a thought, a lifetime of memories locked away in photographs and videos and my mind. My big brother no longer in the room makes the air stifling when I attempt to breathe on my own. I never thought I had any secrets; how could I? We were together so often that there was nothing to hide. I never would have thought that *you* would become my secret.

At Maamaa's suggestion, I have started volunteering to fill up more of my time. To have something outside of working at the shop or my school work. Something that helps others.

Although, I would argue that I am coping well, much better than she seems to think I am. I stay busy with school or work and do not think about you, and if I do, I write a letter. It has almost become a diary of sorts. Either way, I am doing fine. Still, I started at the addiction treatment center yesterday.

It is odd being at the center that you would have been at. The workers recognized me from the day we did a walk-through tour with our parents, but they keep a low profile about it. No sense in telling the patients that one of their activity volunteers could have had a sibling in the very program spot they are in. Being there has brought back a few memories of your last year that I would otherwise prefer to ignore on the back shelf of my mind, but I like the patients.

I will hold art classes on Sundays to help those in recovery. I wonder if taking these types of classes would have helped you. Most likely not, you always were more of a poet.

I am sad to say, Brother,

That the truth is, I haven't picked up a paint brush since senior art. The compulsion to create used to be a second nature to me. I had sketchbooks filled with future works and panel binders full of paintings, dried but not quite completed. For a moment, I wanted to be an artist. To one day have a gallery full of my own pieces, waiting to be transferred to the wall of a person that could afford luxurious art. Maybe I would donate a piece for a charity auction, and it would become someone's tax write-off.

And yet, there was that unspoken threat.

You can't make a living off of art. Go to school graduate get student loans go to school graduate get a job buy a house spend your lifetime paying off the mortgage.

I tried to ignore the thoughts in my brain that told me I would never make it, tried to ignore the strain in people's eyes when I said the words *I want to be an artist.* But it never worked. I gave in to the unspoken pressure and focused on achieving grades good enough to attend some type of postsecondary (although I'd had no plans to go if I could avoid it). At some point, my toolbox dwindled to a few old poorly rinsed brushes, and I stopped replacing the empty spaces.

You never got to see my last painting.

It wasn't a recreational piece. We had senior art slotted for the final semester and it was my one freeing time in the day to lose myself.

The culminating project was told to us ahead of time: Choose an existing assignment made in this class and create the necessary artist statements for the end of year showing. I chose the "Trip Down Memory Lane" assignment.

The plan was to follow a picture from when we were kids, playing in the sandbox together at the park with the toys left behind by the other distracted children. I had it in my head that I would try to make the photo as realistic as I possibly could, wanting to dedicate as much effort as possible into recreating the memory of when the sand wasps stung my ear, and you made me feel better by saying they thought I was a flower.

I spent most of my lunches in the art room, trying to perfect this piece. I couldn't bring myself to detail the faces. They remained empty without features while the rest of the picture was in focus and detailed.

Originally, I had no plan to use it for my culminating nor to display it, but Mr. Vanders encouraged me. As usual, I didn't tell MaamaaBaabaa that I won an art award and took the piece home with me (wanting to toss it in the dumpster), but Baabaa was still in the shop when I came home that night.

He absolutely loved it, and before I could attempt to protest, he was dusting off the gift wrap we stash for the holiday buyers and wrapping it up for Maamaa's upcoming birthday. She loved it and it hangs in the shop above the old couches now.

You and Me,

We always were the artistic duo. You had a way with words, and I had a way of conveying emotion with colors. It was the same with MaamaaBaabaa.

Maamaa was all about books and one day writing her own. I like to think that she will publish that one novel she has been redrafting all our lives.

Baabaa has always been in love with any art medium he could get his hands on.

He taught me how to hold a brush before I could hold a pencil. Maamaa did the opposite with you.

You always mused about publishing your own work and stocking it behind the cash desk with the workers' picks. Always insisting you would one day have your scribblings out for public consumption. You never even let me read them; I could never understand how you could let complete strangers read your innermost thoughts. If you had left me so much as a notebook of scribblings, maybe I could fulfill your life's wish.

Who knows? Maybe you did leave me something hidden on your side of the room.

My art was harder to hide, decorating the walls of the apartment and the shop. I let you see the inner workings of my mind and yet you never gave me the blessing to do the same to you.

That is another new thing for me: I have never had my own room.

When MaamaaBaabaa bought the building, a young urban Indigenous couple full of dreams for their future, it consisted of an old coffee shop downstairs and a two bedroom on the second story. They sold the café equipment in favor of Maamaa's dream for a secondhand bookstore. They had only planned for one child when the decision was made to purchase it. For a long time, the room sat empty except for a rocking chair in the corner as MaamaaBaabaa were busy raising their shop baby and being unsuccessful at creating flesh and blood. The doctors later told Maamaa that they'd been preparing to tell her that she might never conceive, and then, there you were.

A crib was added to the room and the walls were washed green. My arrival so soon after you posed an issue. They could have tried to rent out the apartment and find a new place to accommodate the bodies in the family, but it was ruled out as *too far away, too expensive.* We stayed in the apartment. MaamaaBaabaa were planning on making the living room theirs and giving us each a room (and supposedly they did for a time). That was until they discovered you had crawled out of your bedroom one night and climbed into my crib. From then on out you refused to sleep in a room that I was not in.

Over time the crib and mattress on the floor became two singles on either side of the slim room. Well, they were intended to be on either side of the room. We pushed them together to create one bigger bed until we were sixteen.

Even when we finally had our own beds, we could rarely go a month without sharing with the other. It had become a part of us. Always needing to be lulled to sleep with the sounds of breathing, the held hands. It was very unusual and quite codependent, but it was the way we were. We came as a package deal until we could no longer be.

After the crime scene was cleared and the professional cleaner was done, I had thought of making it my own room before the world truly came crashing down. A different color on the walls maybe? I don't know what my favorite color is; I always just wore what was in our closet. A new bed? It would be a waste to get rid of two perfectly good mattresses. Perhaps I could get a new bedspread to change things up without a permanent change, but the quilts left rumpled on the singles for the last few months are made from our shirts as children.

As quick as the idea of a fresh start (my own room) came, it vanished, and I had to hold my breath. There was no way I could change the room we shared for seventeen years. I fought and screamed when I found something out of place. Quickly, only *I* was allowed access to the room on the left. Anyone else that got in could take or move things and I wanted to preserve the tomb. Baabaa was disappointed when he saw I put a new lock on the door that had never been there before.

Although we always came as a package, that package deal quickly ran out. I thought we would have years, no, decades left to be Ally and Andy. Soon, we were supposed to be the duo with the addition of significant others and one day the addition of children. Business partners at the shop and weekend brunches at each other's houses to catch up on our lives outside of work. Placing bets on whose hair would turn silver first, who would begin to lose their senses, and which one would go first in death. So much of life was robbed from us. We had a whole life ahead of us and it was stolen from you, stolen from us.

I had envisioned us both without pigment in our long hair, still mirroring each other so much that the only difference between us would be our clothing. We would be happy and fat and wrinkled from a lifetime of love and contentment.

I stopped thinking about how old I would become in the future and tried to stop thinking of the future altogether. There was no future without you in it by my side. The future I had wanted was stolen the second your thread was cut.

Sometimes I think of how easy it must have been to die. I imagine it hurts, but after the brain begins to shut down, it must feel like nothing. One second you're there and the next you're gone forever. If I didn't know it'd ruin our parents forever, maybe I would have followed you.

Dear Brother,

I try to push the thoughts away. I try to move on, I really do. Most days, I can go until noon without thinking of you. On some it is not until I come home late at night that I remember. Until I see the green room.

We really should not have kept track of our growth on the doorway of the room. The hallway light reflects off the graphite embedded in the wood, and it explodes the memories I try to keep at bay. Using the apartment and the shop as our personal playground, playdates with Krish, birthdays, and just plain life with a sibling. It is even harder in the room. I have not been able to bring myself to go through your things and clear it out. Currently, it is being used as a storage room for our clothing. I go in quickly, lungs closed off, and grab the nearest thing I see before I run back out and pocket the key.

I have found that I cannot sleep by myself. I have taken to camping out on the floor of MaamaaBaabaa's room. I am aware that I am imposing on them, but I cannot sleep in the room you died in, much less the room full of your earthly things. For a while there I was sleeping on the couch, but Baabaa wouldn't let me anymore after he discovered I was watching shows instead of sleeping for days on end.

Somedays all I want to do is toss everything you owned into a trash bag and leave it in a restaurant dumpster. Make the room my own with no reminders of you. I refrain from giving in to this impulse by reminding myself that you had a lot of nice material things and others could use them. One day I will find the courage to go through everything and create my own space for the first time in my life.

That day is extremely far away. It may be years before I can stand in the room and allow myself to breathe. For now, I will stay on the floor and reuse the same dozen articles of clothing in my bin unless I absolutely need something.

Enough of that. I am supposed to be moving on, not fixating on *what could have been* and *what was.* I need to focus on the living and allow myself to be a part of it. Nothing good will come of wallowing in my own sadness and hiding from others.

I have filled my upcoming week full of things to do. A good ratio of working, school, volunteering, and friends. It is still weird to believe that I have *friends.* Do not get me wrong, I am still in contact with Krish, and we talk several times a week, but it is different being able to see and touch those around you.

James is planning on hosting a party on Friday night and I intend to go. I have never been much of a drinker, and especially now I am taking those silly DARE oaths we made as children to the police seriously, but it will be nice to get out and meet more people.

I am maintaining my usual work schedule of evenings and weekends. Baabaa started taking me on restock pickups when we need it now. I like finding something new in the garages and lawns of others, but I also like standing behind the counter and the customers. I get more time to do my homework if I am not stocking the shelves.

My first day of volunteering was a little awkward. I felt under-qualified standing in front of the patients while they all stared, waiting for me to begin instruction. I don't think I could have been a teacher. I've only ever worked customer service and it is what I'm best at. So, I plastered on a smile and started using my customer service voice.

A brief introduction: *Hello! My name is Andy, and I am a painter. It helps me cope when I need it and so we thought it would be an easy hobby for you to develop during your stay! Shall we begin?* I kept using my hands to speak so my sleeve would fall and I could read the ink prompts on my wrist. We began with their favorite three colors and their favorite plant. I encouraged the group to think of the common colors in their closet if they were unsure of their favorites. Not everyone knew their favorite plant so next week we are going to the courtyard where they can find a plant that resonates with them. I have found that I enjoy volunteering.

But as for the party, my stomach starts to sink with dread, and I feel as if I am being forced to attend prom. I don't want to annoy Delilah or James by shadowing them all night and yet I am uncomfortable with the idea of striking up a conversation with a complete stranger. You were always the more outgoing of us.

To my Brother,

No matter how uncomfortable or anxiety fueled, it is almost exciting to learn how to navigate life on my own. Even doing the shopping on my own is an adventure.

I have taken to people-watching. I create lives for the strangers that I interact with in my head. Everything goes by much faster when I am able to do exactly what needs to be done with no one to get sidetracked by every five seconds. That does not mean that I am entirely content on my own. I grew up with a constant companion; I still need one to cope throughout the day. Delilah is perfect for this. She is able to pick up on my current emotion and knows how to make me feel better or distract me if needed. We are with each other so often these days that MaamaaBaabaa want to meet her, but I like having her to myself.

She is easily becoming my best friend. My first best friend that is entirely my own. There are times that I forget she has never known you and almost slip up. I am so used to being one side of a coin that having people who do not know you is more often uncomfortable than a relief. Sometimes I want to tell her about you. Tell her that once upon a time there was a male counterpart to me, but most days, I do not have the mental energy to explain that I lost my other half less than a year ago.

I wish I had the energy. There are so many stories to tell I do not know where to start. I could begin with the more innocent, such as when we would fill sleeping bags with blankets and fall down the stairs. Or the time before we grew too tall, and we tried to climb the bookshelves and step between them without knocking them over. I could tell her of the color Baabaa's face turned when he found you under a bookshelf.

I don't think I could tell her the personal things, the more secretive. I have not told a soul that I knew what you were up to. That I knew you were not well, but I took your lies at face value and believed you were going through a destructive cycle that would be short-lived. I do not think I could tell Delilah that because of me, you were short-lived.

Dearly Departed,

Yes, I am a cliché. Yes, I believe it is my fault. That is because it is *true.*

If it weren't for my covering for you, perhaps you would have gotten the help you needed sooner.

If it weren't for my faith that you could get better with only me to keep you here, perhaps you would have had that same faith in me being enough to keep you tethered to our life.

If it weren't for me, perhaps you would still be alive.

Brother, I also believe

I believe Delilah can sense that there is something off about me. She can sense that something is missing from me. She's right, there is *someone* missing.

It feels like the days after you died when I could not eat. I am so hollow and empty that I could reach down my throat and pull out my organs one at a time. I have no light anymore. I was always your mirror, your reflection. I think the candlelight I used to burn inside was instead a poor reflection of your sun.

There are times when she stares at me so intently that it is as if she can see my splintered spirit. Baabaa mentioned one day that he saw my inner being shatter when I looked into the room that day. He had tried to pin me against the wall. With each scream and cry that caused my voice to go hoarse and eventually disappear, a piece of me was sent spiraling into the cosmos. I was never whole on my own and now the broken pieces of my spirit search for you.

She has yet to ask what is wrong, for which I am eternally grateful. For now, it is nice to play pretend. I pretend I am a person who is whole and socialize as if my life is not missing a vital person. I believe she can see through it, see through the sheet I hide behind, but knows I am not ready to tell her.

I am sorry, Brother,

When life changes so quickly and nothing is normal, nothing is home, all I want is my person back. I want life to be the way it was before, but I cannot raise the dead and life will never be the way it was before. All I want is to be a person with regular coping mechanisms, instead of using another person as one.

I want to be a person that relishes the feeling of an empty stomach, hides within the smoke-filled lungs, that rush of pain and endorphins as your skin divides. All I want is some form of habit to help me survive. I wish I was a person that could jump from extreme heights with complete faith in a cord that would be my lifeline. I wish I could fit in our tiny tub and feel myself centering and becoming present with the warm, bubbly liquid caressing my body and the scent of candles in the air. I wish I got a rush from purchasing something, anything. I would trade my college savings if it meant shopping would fill this hole inside. I do not care whether it is destructive or something that is too expensive to rationalize using any of it. I need something to help me go through the days that are so suffocating I cannot open my mouth. I need to not need it.

I never had a need for a habit to help me cope; I always had a person. When things became too much, my mirror would squeeze me tight and level my vision. It was a warm hand in mine. The ramblings of the day, the weather, the customer that bought the whole shelf of a certain author, anything to make the denseness clear. I have never been one for harmful coping mechanisms; I have always been one to put my all into one person to keep me afloat.

It is a tricky thing, living this way. You put everything you have in one person and trust them to always be there to always make you feel well. What do you do when that person is gone and has returned to the *gitchi-manitoo*? That is my question of the day.

Alas, Brother,

I am not used to being my own person yet. Much less being alone. Delilah helps but I feel as if I poison her presence if I am around her too much. The emptiness inside me is a void that wants to swallow everything and anything.

That emptiness inside was created when our threads severed. I need a patch for the ripped hole. I need another person, someone to connect with on a level that I am not afraid of ruining. You were once that person for me, but I think it is time to explore another one.

Krish's parting words to me were to find someone, someone to help me in the ways he cannot. For a brief time after you were gone, Krish became the person I needed. We banded together as those that feel the pain of an empty seat in a booth, those that could understand the Ally-sized hole left within my being.

I say brief time because he left me too. I know he did not want to.

He spoke of staying home and working at the restaurant, but I knew that was not what he genuinely wanted. He wanted to see what else was there in the world and to study what he loves. The family business was not his calling as it was mine. In the end, he left, and I made a promise to find something, someone to make me feel normal.

I could tell it hurt him to tell me this. Even hundreds of kilometers away he tries to be the person I need but the distance makes it hard. Our schedules make it hard to always be with each other. I told him to find what he needs to heal, and I think it is my time to find who I need in order to heal.

To Ally,

This is where it gets interesting. There are so many people on campus, so many people captivated by Delilah's essence that I meet so many unknown faces. There are so many possibilities. That is the beautiful thing about paying to be in a community filled with numerous cultures and identities. I take cues from Delilah. Flash a smile and nod along like you remember their name after they uttered it so fast you were still looking at the smudge of eyeliner under a watery eye. I have thought about blind dates or dating apps, but I do not want to be one of my missing sisters.

It is a game of attraction. What do they notice first? Does their voice stay the same pitch as they turn to address me? I borrow clothing from Delilah to play a different person. I become someone I do not think I am and stop myself as my eyes begin to scan for my face in the crowd. I find myself looking for someone that fits every invisible criterion I create in my head.

I know, Brother, I know,

Treating it as an equation is perhaps not what I should do. Perhaps I should be reckless and not look for a specific person but find myself within other people. Or I could stop caring so much. Delilah says love comes to you when you are not searching for it. Do I want love, or do I want someone to make my head work right? Things are changing so fast these days. Who is to say that I will not find the one when I am not looking? Do I even want the "one"?

Dear Brother,

Occasionally, I get so confused that I am unable to complete a sentence when there is no one else to finish it for me. Life becomes entirely too much some days and I hide in MaamaaBaabaa's closet like I am three again. Playing hide and seek with reality. Eventually she pulls me out and gives me a task to do so I will be useful. Today I did not hide. Today I did all my chores. I did the new inventory. I made *dinner.*

Baabaa asked what I wanted so bad. "Will there be drugs?" Maamaa asked, completely ignoring my plea to spend the night at Delilah's.

I assured her that it is a chance to meet the others on campus row. I have no desire to do drugs, or drink. MaamaaBaabaa don't drink. I have never tried it. They know this, and I know that because of you, they are afraid that I may follow in your footsteps. My head is so messed up when I am sober, who knows what it would be like if I were under the influence? Besides, I keep *my* promises.

Oh, Brother of Mine,

There is so much to tell.

I want to tell you all about it in a whirlwind. I raced up the back stairs to the room, for a moment fully expecting you to be sleeping the day away. I will have to settle for writing it out in letters that can never reach their addressee.

The party was not really a party in my opinion. Nothing like the bangers on film. Just a few people milling around the room, James's record collection playing in the background. Delilah introduced me to a range of people in her class, her program, his class, his program. A few faces I recognized, but none whose names were worth remembering. I stuck near Helena for most of the evening. Delilah absolutely loves party games and somehow made them fun.

Helena stated herself my partner for the night and we dominated. Where I was lost within the game, she could find me, and vice versa. As the night went on, I began to see Helena in a different light. She was no longer the girl I sat next to in my English class that I went to a museum with one time, instead she became a person to me.

Dear Brother,

We just kept talking. It is easy to talk with her. Soon enough people were leaving the apartment and we were still chattering away. Delilah interrupted us at one point to ask if we were still staying the night.

"I don't really want the night to end, do you, Andy?" Helena smiled and I felt this warmth within me. I would have followed her to the end of worlds if she asked.

Instead, I followed her to the dorms.

Brother,

You can tell a lot about a person from their room. It is full of their essence and emotions. The rumpled bedding, the finished candles on the windowsill, books left open. In Helena's case, there were a lot of textbooks perfectly stacked on the desk, binders color coded per class, photos of family on the wall. She is studying to be a radiology tech, planning to go back home to a little hospital town.

I quickly learned Helena is very organized and full of dreams. A person with a sense of purpose and fully dedicated to her goals. She knows exactly who she is.

Maybe her confidence will wear off on me.

I am six again. Sitting on the edge of an unfamiliar bed in a building I have never been in. A friend of a friend is milling around, pointing out their different possessions.

I got this at camp, I turned it into a pillow after I ripped off the sleeves.

There is brown against the gray walls of a filled corkboard. There is a schedule in a print so small I almost think I really should wear my glasses more often. There are pictures taped to the cork; not family pictures, no, it is a collage. Helena shows me the box under her bed.

She takes the magazines from the recycling bins and makes mood boards. Some are the same color, some are mosaics of different lives. I sit and watch as she adjusts the stick glue to a piece of paper.

I feel warm. The window has been open, and it is no longer summer. The weather is changing. The leaves are a mix of browns and greens. A girl is sitting on the carpet making a mess. She smiles and brushes a fallen hair into place. Stickers get stuck in her hair and she does not care. Her fingers push down the ripped magazines and burst the bubbles.

I find myself crossing the room to the photos on the other walls. There are so many of them, not just scenery pictures but people with the same grins. I try to count and lose the number every time I see a new picture. She tells me she has so many cousins she sees them as siblings. Rattles off the names so fast I don't catch any of them. She has a hamster back home that the littlest one isn't allowed to hold anymore. I tell her I have never had a pet and she thinks it is the funniest thing in the world. Before I know it, we are laughing together. Laughing at the little hamster that prefers to live in the laundry room over his cage and the stickers in her hair. I feel warm and for once I find the warmth reaching my smile.

Her round cheeks cut deep with dimples and brown lipstick; she asks if I wear lipstick. I say no I don't like the feeling of things on my lips. She outlines them with a sticky finger. I can taste the glue.

It reminds me of kindergarten, a time when we made papier-mâché and collage artwork out of the receipts after tax periods.

She smells like cinnamon. There's no candle burning but she smells like apples and cinnamon and the warmth spreads to my chest. We sit in silence. I feel like I am on fire. I am afraid to open my mouth in fear of becoming a fire-breathing dragon like the one on her mood board and burning everything to ash.

Her hand is cold. When it is in mine, it becomes the conductor of my fire, and she leans closer to me. My fire becomes her heater, and I cannot stay away.

I see the dips and rises in her brown eyes. If we were lit by sunlight and not a desk lamp, I know there would be gold in those beautiful eyes. Her now warm hands outline my jaw, my cheekbones.

"I wish I was so angular."

I tell her she's beautiful.

She says thank you and dimples again. I want to kiss those dimples. I do.

The fire reaches my veins, and I am no longer myself. Or at least the me I thought I knew. I am daring and new.

My hands are in her hair. She is pulling out my braid after asking permission. Fingertips running along soft flesh, teeth clinking, uncoordinated movements.

"Is this okay?" She repeats it so much I just have to shut her up with my mouth.

Yes, yes, yes.

I feel like I am in grade eleven again, unnerved, and full of angst and hormones and needing another person.

I give her my fire and we burn together.

Truly Brother,

I have never given much thought about my sexuality. In fact, I have never given anything regarding such matters any thought. Past experiences have made me believe I was straight. That I preferred male over female but that seems to not be the case. Helena has awakened something that I never had the nerve to discover.

I was always the reserved one. The one that was perfectly content to hide away in a shell and allow life to pass me by. I took what came my way and never bothered to try anything new. Anything different.

This was different. *This was new.* I had never taken the time to ponder about my sexuality. After all, you had to care about your life enough to ask yourself the big questions. I never cared enough to change the path that was laid out for me.

I was to run the shop in partner with you and perhaps one day provide grandchildren. What happened between those life milestones never piqued my interest. But now it has to.

Could I be the girl that turns gay after one night?

Falling helplessly for the first girl to brush my lips, aching for the soft body beneath my fingertips, replaying that one night over and over until it becomes the broken record I was always destined to be?

It could have been hiding inside me for years until I was ready to go on an adventure. I believe it was.

I believe it was nested comfortably in the marrow of my bones, racing from joint to joint, bouncing around with my blood cells. Eager to be let out to play. Preparing to bring electricity to my fingertips, to my lips. It was not a conscious decision. I simply reacted. The otherness inside crashed against the glass of my bones and broke out to have a hand at the game of hearts.

We finally exchanged numbers the next morning and I see that number every day. We text so often Maamaa thinks I have a boyfriend. It is my little secret to know it is a girl.

We eat lunch together between classes and spend evenings in her dorm or walking through the parks. Most days Delilah and James are with us; other days it is just us. I like our time alone. When we are alone together it feels like we are just friends but a secret part inside me knows we are not. We are something more and I think she can see it in my eyes.

I am growing used to physical touch again. I hold hands with my friends and my not so friend. I forget the days when I would hold a hand that was identical to mine and now relish in the different tones in contrast against my skin. We hold each other and cuddle in ways I never have with friends, even my not so friend from before. They feel like a family to me, one that does not fall apart so easily.

It is a new sensation to get *used* to things again. I am getting used to smiling without force. I am getting used to going out for more than just classes. I am getting used to living again but I have never lived this way.

It is all new. I have friends of my own. I am falling in love with my art again because I can see how it helps the patients. I am seeing art in everything again: in the changing of leaves, in the oily soup filled with vegetables, in the pink of her cheeks. I am carrying a sketchbook now; my homework is so full of my mindless doodles that I decided I might as well keep some for myself. My bag is heavy with this letter book and my sketches but I feel calm with them in my possession at all times. I feel calm and I feel alive.

Alas Brother,

All days are not the same. Some days I can see the sunshine and the spark in others. Other days I see the thick clouds and the sadness in their eyes.

I feel alive but feeling alive again means you feel other things. I am not coasting through life anymore. I make decisions and I am so easily overwhelmed with making decisions. I cannot watch new shows anymore; there is so much to choose from so I watch the same comfort shows over and over again.

I want to paint the room and make it my own but I cannot decide what to do with your things and then I do not want to get rid of any of it; I want to keep it for myself and keep a shrine in a sacred space but there is no space for that. You have no room anymore; your worldly objects take up so much space and I want to throw them out the window and count the people that get hit.

Dear Brother,

Taking advantage of our Monday afternoon classes, I have started spending the night in Helena's dorm and we grab breakfast in the cafeteria. She has a mandatory meal plan with the college (for staying in residence), and I'd rather not toil at home waiting for my classes to begin.

We sit near the windows and take in the autumn views. I have grown comfortable with holding her hand while we wait in line and not letting go unless we need utensils to eat. Her hands are forever cold, and I wish I never gave up learning to knit; I would love to gift her a pair of mittens.

There have only been a few times of us sleeping in and grabbing a late morning meal but every weekend I find myself looking forward to it. I feel as if I am defrosting when I am with her. Things are easier and continue to improve with each waking day. Mondays are the only days I sleep more than a few hours and find myself blinking into the late morning sun.

Maybe it is the fact that I am finally sleeping on a semi-regular schedule or maybe it is just having Helena in my life now. She has become my lifeline and I am eternally grateful.

Helena is surprised I have never had my own room.

She thinks I also have a big family for whatever reason but also thinks we all had our own spaces. I tell her no I shared it with my brother before I could stop myself.

She says nothing but her eyes are so intense I know it is that time when she is waiting for me to continue. I tell her we shared everything — clothes, friends, a room. I have never had anything of my own and now I do.

She does not ask what happened to you and for that I am also grateful.

A part of me wishes she would ask. She did not say anything after I briefly explained my dead sibling and I wish she would. I wish I could tell her all of the highlights of your life, just to provide a taste of what *I* would be like if you were still here.

I want to tell her of the time you fancied yourself a bard and tried reciting poetry in the park at ten years old. I want to tell her of when we couldn't find our step stool for the shop counter, so you managed to convince *me* to be the stool until Maamaa asked where I was. I want to tell her of when we passed by a man sitting out in the cold and you took off your brand-new winter coat for him.

There are so many memories of the life I had before and they are all filled with you. I would share them if only she would ask.

She starts lending me clothes. They are too big and a bit short, but I start using Baabaa's belts to make them fit. The pile of clothes on your side of the room builds.

Soon enough, I no longer wear our clothes and I am only wearing hers. They are a little big and short, but it makes me feel loved to have the honor of wearing her clothing. She showed me how to accessorize and make the ill-fitting clothing look fashionable rather than awkward. She is constantly playing with my waist-length hair and watching tutorials on how to do more than my simple double braids.

I see someone else in the mirror when I look now. I don't see my brother; I see myself. I haven't decided if I like being myself yet. I am still learning who this new person is.

Dear Brother,

The weather is changing to the way you liked it best. Decay is in the chilled air, and I've started wearing your jacket to keep warm. I know I said I was done wearing your clothes, but the jacket is nice, and it was originally mine before you took it. Maamaa looked sad when she saw me leave the house in your jacket, but she smiled when I said where I was going.

We piled into Delilah's car and drove toward the mountains. Past the city's borders and past the cows, down the long road to the pumpkin patches. I haven't been since we were young, and it hasn't changed much. The company did change though. I liked sitting in the back with Helena's hand in mine. She kept putting leaves in her hair and it looked so beautiful.

It was muddy but the sun was out. We did the monster corn maze, shot at the scarecrow, took pictures in the barn, and rode the wagons. It was simple but a wonderful way to spend the chilly day.

We rode home with pumpkins in our laps and spent the evening hollowing the insides and daring each other to eat the stringy bits. James showed us how to bake the squash and Helena roasted seeds.

There is so much calm in the air when we are all together. I can see myself staying friends with these people until we start seeing gray hairs.

Guess what, Ally?

I invited Helena over for the harvest. She did not want to go home, and everyone already left this morning, went back home to the surgeons and nurses. Baabaa is planning to go all out this year. He has me prebaking and redoing grocery list after grocery list.

Maamaa pesters over hearing more about Helena. Wants to know everything there is to know about the girl that lights up my eyes. Baabaa is simply happy I am getting close to people again.

Dear Brother,

I will admit I was mildly anxious about telling our parents that I invited my *girlfriend* over for dinner. Not in a get kicked out for suggesting it way, but as a family it was never discussed if anyone would turn out non-heteronormative conforming. Part of me always wondered if they thought I was nonbinary due to our constant sharing of clothing and mirror imaging of each other, especially after shows started having more representation and we had to explain for them to understand.

We were in the kitchen on Saturday morning preparing to go for our weekly book haul. Baabaa was making sure we had enough boxes and Maamaa was going over the list of donations we received that week and which local initiative the proceeds should go to for the new quarter. I was standing by the coffee pot, both willing it to drip faster so we could leave and willing it to slow down so I could work on how I was going to come out.

In the end, I filled all three thermoses with blends exactly the way they like them and decided to pull a bit of flair out of your life. *MaamaaBaabaa can my girlfriend come for dinner with us next week?* I asked, putting the thermoses in front of them as if I were asking about the weather.

"Which one? Delilah or Helena?" Maamaa asked, not looking up from her lists.

Not a girl friend, Maamaa ... Helena is my girlfriend.

"Yes, I am aware you have friends, which one are you bringing?"

Baabaa laughed softly at her. "Lorraine, I think Andria is telling us she is gay."

That made her look up, a slight scowl on her face. "Of course you are. Now, which friend of yours is the special friend?"

My nerves melted away and I cleared up any remaining obtuseness Maamaa had. She said she'd love to meet the girl that has me smiling again and shooed us away to get on with our work. In the truck, Baabaa gave my shoulder a good squeeze with the slight shimmer back in his eyes.

The harvest is tomorrow, and I am thinking of asking Helena to come over more than just for dinner. To come again the next day.

I have decided I want my own room. I am going to bare it all and show her your shrine. Take everyone's advice on claiming the room as my own and get her help with redecorating. I still don't know what I am like on my own and I need her help to figure that out.

I took her hand and showcased the lives that no one has seen since the party. The apartment was alive again. She laughed at Baabaa's jokes and Maamaa smiled at me over her shoulder. We ate and joked and pretended to not notice when I sat in your chair because I could not bear for her to take it.

Her eyes did not change when she saw the pictures on the walls. When she saw there used to be two of us. Her smile is so warm I want to ignore summer and heat myself with its temperature. I prepared myself for the questions, but I did not expect complete kindness.

I decided she deserved to know. After dinner I brought her to our room and watched anxiously as she examined the space. Two beds, two trunks, one closet of clothes. Your various trinkets. She handled everything with grace, touching with the flutter of a bird, a blank but knowing expression.

I told her the story of my brother Alexander. The Ally to my Andy. My twin from different births. She listened with bright eyes. After my tale ended in death, she had one question: "Can you live a life that is entirely your own?"

Dear Alex,

Her question rang through my ears for days.

I want a life of my own. I want to be a person, not the shadow that is all that is left. I want to build a life that is not spent thinking of what was lost. I asked her to help me.

We started early the next morning. We took the empty boxes from the alley and filled them with ~~our~~ your things. I never realized how little of the room was truly in my ownership. It is so bare now. All the closet space in the world, my trunk more than half empty, nothing on the surfaces. It feels eerie, like you are finally dead.

But we found something.

She declared that we had to deeply clean the room. To purge it of any remaining essence. I was the only one that would fit and crawled under the beds. Under my bed, I found a shoebox. A box filled with loose paper and half-empty notebooks. Broken crayons and bitten pens. The content filled with sprawling scribblings of words.

We found your poems.

Alex,

I have yet to bring myself to read them all. Instead, they sit vigil on your bed. Funny of you to hide such an important box under my bed. A present (or horror) from the beyond right where I could not sleep for months. I want to read it, but I am afraid of what it might contain.

Maybe you think no one noticed at first but I did. I saw your decline. I was never away from your side for more than a few hours; how could I not have noticed? In truth, I was afraid of you. What you were becoming. I waited it out. Thought that you would become the Ally I knew from before the drugs.

Your decline was odd. First, you began to quiet and shrink in on yourself. I became the one that had to stand in your sunlight when you dimmed. And then you became better. Sunny again. Not as bright but light all the same. And then it dropped again. I could feel your agitation and your indecision. Just before I was finally ready to ask what was going on, you began to radiate. So bright and fast it felt like we were kids again. No one noticed the change because I mirrored it as always. But I noticed and I tried my best.

To Alex,

Delilah took me shopping when she got back as an apology for not being able to attend the dinner. (She just wanted an excuse to dress me up in clothing that actually fit.) I could have brought your things to drop at the charity shops we went to, but I am not ready to let go yet. I would rather have your things in boxes if it means they are still in our room.

She financed the afternoon despite my protests and took it as power to dress me in everything she found suitable.

It was fun. I never got the chance to have a real girl friend that I would go shopping or play dress up with. Helena doesn't count; she *is* my girlfriend.

Delilah talked nonstop while maintaining the calming vibe as always. She spoke of her multiple cousins and aunties and uncles and her surgeon parents that only get this previous holiday off. She spoke of thinking of getting implants one day to appear more feminine in her waxed chest. I assured her she does not need them if she already feels comfortable the way she currently is.

We bonded more today than we had before.

I know I have been spending the majority of my time alone with Helena and it was a nice change. It made me feel normal, especially when she asked for details about Helena's and my relationship. I said it was new, but it felt intense, and I hoped she felt the same way. I felt like a schoolgirl in movies, wondering if the person I'm seeing likes me back.

We ended the day with greasy food and some clothing of my own for once.

Dear Brother, I need advice:

I haven't given much thought to what Helena and I are. Is she truly my girlfriend?

Maamaa thinks so. Says she does not care as long as I'm happy. Says I look happier when she's around. My light is back on when she is near.

Baabaa says love looks good in my dark eyes. Is it love? He says it is, clear as day, he can see it. First love stays in your heart forever, he says, and if you're lucky, they stay with you forever.

I would like to have what MaamaaBaabaa have with Helena. I can't plan a life for us though; I need to take time to think about our relationship and see if it really is what MaamaaBaa think it is.

I have never been in love before. How can I know if I love her?

Brother, did you love?

I see love all around me. The love for our parents, the love they have for each other. The love of friendship between James and Delilah. The love they have for me.

I see it in the customers. The tender way they hold a long-searched-for novel. The gentle nudge and smile as they point to their favorite section. The light in a person's eyes as they stand in the corner where they think I cannot see them, but they do not care because they love the book so much.

I see it in movies, in poetry, in the novels I stock. I see it in everything, but I do not see it as something for me.

There is love available for me. People love me. This I know, but what I do not know is how to love and how to be loved.

Dear Brother,

Now that love is on my mind I am trying to trace back when Helena and I first got together (does that count as an anniversary or does it have to be a date?) and romantic-themed holidays.

We were in fifth grade when our classmates moved on from the childhood minute-crushes to make-believe. Every three days or so there was a new one popping up between friends or bursting. I found it hard to keep track of who was with who, and by the time I finally got it understood, they weren't together anymore.

Except Jack and Kayleigh of course. They went down south to the same university this year. Together since fifth grade, I can hardly believe it! Best wishes to them.

Remember how I said yes to the one boy who ended up moving a month later? We never did break up, so maybe I'm still with him.

Anyway, Valentine's Day was a big deal that year. Suddenly everyone was very coordinated with who got which card out of the character packets from the department store and you got quite a few in your brown bag mailbox. They all had the little heart stickers and a few had a home phone number on them. You found it ridiculous because any girl that wanted you might as well have wanted me with how much we looked alike. I tried convincing you that maybe one of the girls would make you happy like Trevor made me (sometimes I wonder if Trevor found out he really wanted *you* and not *me*) but you were having none of it.

In your eyes, everyone was a friend and friends didn't need to be more than that. You went as far as reminding everyone of the lesson we got the previous year on the origins of Valentine's Day. It was a yearly reminder of the Romans forcing enlistment by forbidding marriages, and a Saint who went on to hold them in private and later was beheaded.

The concept of romance was lost on you, and yet I wish I could tell you about the way Helena's touch makes my heart swell and her smile makes my breath catch. If I could fill her university mailbox with a "Be My Valentine?" card with the heart stickers and the heart-shaped suckers that taste vaguely of butter, I would, but those won't be in stores for a few more months.

Maybe I'll do a special crafted bag like we did in elementary school for the occasion in the new year. Or I could reuse a previous one — I'm sure Maamaa still has our school crafts in that filing cabinet in her closet, but you always were better with glue.

Dear Brother,

A few months back, we implemented a weekly question we'd ask the customers as we rang up their findings. It is displayed on the blackboard with the available discounts and staff picks. Either the customer sees it and asks first, or we ask. I chose this week's: "Are you in love?" (The current staff pick is an assortment of novels that heavily feature romance, not that it isn't helping me as well ...)

One person was in the store when I started my shift after school today. The same old man that regularly drops off book donations and fills the charity jar. (It was decided that proceeds for this quarter would go to the Family Center's Food Box program.) I tidied the counter while I waited on his milling around the sections. He came to the till with a stack of books we picked up last Saturday morning and asked the question, the same way he always does when he comes in on Wednesdays.

"My dear, are you in love?"

I hope to be. Are you?

"I am in love every day, with everything."

That's beautiful. It'll be forty with your discount.

"Don't look for ways you can be in love, the truth will find you."

I never told you before, but I always pretend the old man is our grandfather. He is full of wisdom and always leaves too much money and runs for the door before I can correct his "mistake." We never got to meet our grandparents and I pretend he is one of them. A sweet man with so much insight into the world.

Ally,

Did you ever wonder about our grandparents? Who they are and who they could have been? We only knew snippets and never prompted for more. Unknown relatives still plagued with the curse of bottled fire, unknown relatives that never got the chance to be relatives.

It went unspoken in our small family that we did not ask. We could only speak of it if our parents began the conversation but that rarely happened.

Sometimes I stare at the faces of strangers that look like us, some more than others with the same curve of mouth or jawline, and even more that are just strangers with the same unsaid labels plastered to their faces or beige and red laminate cards in wallets (or the fancier white cards).

Maybe we would have done a better job in life if we knew more about who we were and where we came from, who we came from.

Anyway,

I take the old man's advice to heart. I stop looking for ways to be in love and let myself feel.

I listen within when I do this. To the rush of fire in my veins when she touches me. The rush of blood to my face when she winks. The burn in my heart when she gasps. It is all so intense I feel like my candle has become engulfed in flame. I burn so bright around her I become a person I have never been before. I am talkative, I laugh openly and loudly, I dance and sing and live in the moment. I am you without having you around to mirror.

When I come home, to an empty room with filled boxes, my flame dims. I am a gas lamp with the knob turned low. The emptiness and reminders suffocate me and comfort me at the same time. I run from the room you died in with my blanket and pillow in tow, prepared to spend yet another night on the air mattress. I spend this time yearning. I yearn for her body to be against mine, to see her smile and laugh. I yearn for her touch. I yearn for the fuel she adds to the fire raging within.

Ally,

I can breathe around her. I feel whole and not half when I am with her. I am a whole when I am with her. All she knows of you is pictures and left-behind belongings. All she knows of me is my fire and my love. She does not know the brother that outshone me.

We spent the night together again. It is a school night (not Sunday night), but I get to sleep in a tiny bit if I stay on campus, no need for an hour-long bus ride. Truth is, I want to sleep somewhere that you have never touched. The bonus is that she is here. I am surrounded by her things. Her art, her pictures, her overly perfumed candles, her chair of carefully laid clothing.

She is lying in bed as I write at her desk. Her chest rising and falling, hair fanned across her delicate face, pajamas peeking under the blanket. She is serene and she is mine.

I think I love her.

I love her.

I love the way her nose scrunches when she is concentrating hard.

I love the way her eyes light up when she speaks of her family.

I love her kindness and her protectiveness of those she cares for.

I love her and I really hope she loves me too.

Baabaa is right. He is always right.

The old man is right: to love is to love every day and with everything.

I love her today and I loved her yesterday and I will love her tomorrow.

Love is not linear; it grows as time passes and mine can only grow. She fills my heart and my veins to full capacity, and I have to let it out.

I have to tell her. We have been seeing each other for over a month now. She is my girlfriend. If I don't tell her soon, how much longer will she be?

The answer is, she never was.

She never was my girlfriend.

I was never her girlfriend. She never felt love for me; she never felt anything for me.

I was a body to her. A bed warmer. She took my love willingly and refused to reciprocate.

She took my heart and squished out the love and blood. The flames followed the dripping blood and set fire to my clothes, my skin.

I ache and she feels nothing.

I ache and she *wants to be friends.*

I ache and *she never loved me at all.*

Delilah calls it a form of asexuality. A section of the ever-growing rainbow of which I was not aware. Sure, I knew some people had no sexual desire, but I didn't know that was considered sexual orientation.

I especially did not know that another form called aromantic existed. An absence of romantic emotion. More like an absence of human emotion, I say.

Delilah says that I am being cruel. I say my heart is broken and my body was used by someone that didn't bother to lay out the circumstances of our relationship.

The worst part is that she is still in my friend group as if nothing happened.

She tried cornering me in English to tell me she is sorry it has to be this way and I tell her *you are the one that made it this way.*

Add oil to the fire. Watch it burn the rest of me.

Enjoy my body with no feeling of the love I have for you.

The love I *had* for her. How can I continue to love someone that doesn't care about my cracked heart?

I refuse to be around her now.

When I am near her the ache is so strong, I can't breathe.

Not just the ache, the betrayal. She betrayed my trust by neglecting to tell me the truth. She betrayed my trust by taking it from my body and not bothering to realize a heart comes within the body.

I made someone switch unassigned/assigned seats with me. They resisted at first until I explained that she broke my heart. I made excuses to avoid seeing my friends if they told me she was there. They are my friends; how can they choose the person that broke my heart over me?

Delilah is trying to stay in contact with me, but I think she is starting to give up. Everyone gives up on me; I don't see why she shouldn't either. I'm just a piece of cheap clothing that you wear a few times until your aesthetic changes.

I can feel Helena looking at me during class. I grit my teeth and narrow in on the instructor, refusing to drop or flunk a class because of a hurtful girl. I wish she would leave; she's the problem, not me. My only problem was thinking I was worthy of her love and that she was worthy of mine.

Maamaa won't let me run cash anymore. Says I am a short fuse that needs to cool down. I have taken to stocking the shelves and tracking inventory.

It is all I have been doing for the past two weeks. It is repetitive and easy to lose myself in, but I miss the interaction. I miss people watching the customers and making up the weekly question.

I miss who I was when my veins burned, not my skin.

James says I am being unreasonable. That I cannot divide a friend group over a misunderstanding. As if my broken heart is simply a misunderstanding.

If wanting to see my friends without her tainting the space is unreasonable, then fine, I am being unreasonable.

If wanting things to be different is unreasonable, then fine, I am being unreasonable.

If wanting my love to be scrubbed clean and extinguished from my body is unreasonable, then fine, I am being unreasonable.

Dear Brother,

I feel like everyone is walking on eggshells around me. It is worse than it was when we were preparing to send you into detox. I see Maamaa's tightening fist. I see her frustration with me.

Sometimes I want her to hit me. She never has and never would, but I want to feel something other than this pain. I want to trade this pain for something else. But she will not ever hit me. She is just frustrated and digging her nails into her palms because I have closed myself off again.

I am a ghost within the building, hiding between shelves and living under beds. The person they began to know is gone and the people they knew before that are long gone.

I am no one.

Ally,

The one thing I have is my art.

Not really my art. I have yet to touch the small basket of supplies in the back of the closet, but the art of my classes.

I go in every Sunday for one hour and tell the patients to draw an emotion, a feeling. It is supposed to be something that will help their sobriety.

My latest instructions have definitely opened up talking space for their inner issues with the aid of the on-hand counselors. I tell them to create their anger, their aches, their breaks. Before I told them to create what they love.

The pictures on the drying racks are angry and terrifying but they are real.

Brother, I believe

Pain is more real than a mask. I tried to mask my pain over losing you by being under her touch.

I tried to hot glue a papier-mâché mask to my face with the words *I'm fine I'm happy I'm smiling.* I listened to Krish's horrible advice and tried to find someone else to fix the twin-sized space in my insides. He was an okay supplement but reminded me so much of you that it hurt more than his grip did.

The mask works for a while but eventually it burns away. It becomes ash that clings to your raw and bleeding skin. Glitter clogging your pores and cutting into your muscles. All that is left is the pain.

Why hide, why cover, why mask the pain if it is always going to be there?

All this time I have been angry at Helena for breaking my heart.

At my friends for not seeing things from my point of view.

At myself for not being enough.

When all this time, I should have been angry at you.

I spent months agonizing over your death, finding my way under bodies to feel better. Becoming an empty shell that did not know how to live on my own. I left myself, became a husk of what I could have been because I was never able to become my own person.

I was your mirror, and now that mirror is cracked.

It is warped and splintered and sharp. There is no more mirror. Just a broken person left behind by an even more broken brother.

Brother,

I try to put myself into your shoes (in fact I wear your shoes).

I try to imagine losing myself to prescriptions and I can see it. I see how easy it could be to find some way, any way to not feel like this.

I try to imagine how things could have been different. If we were never made to be twins, would life have been easier for us?

Would you have lived?

Would I know how to live?

I want to set your things on fire.

Seeing them makes me so angry. I have finally moved the few things I do have into the living room and made it my space. I sleep on the couch away from our parents and avoid your room. It brings back memories of your last year if I am in there. I cannot sleep in our parents' room anymore. I can't imagine sleeping in your room. I can barely live in the apartment.

Sometimes I sneak down to the store and sleep in there, waking before Maamaa does so I can sneak back in and leave the house before they notice the couch was not slept on.

I'd rather throw your things in the trash than take the care to borrow the truck and drop them off at a charity.

It is more fitting to treat your possessions the same as you treated your life: without a care in the world for the good that could come of it.

I started to push everything into the hallway to bring it to the dumpster when I saw the box on your bed.

Helena helped find that box.

It was shoved so far under my bed it looked like a shadow in the corner when I originally found it. I almost threw it into a bag, ready for tomorrow's trash, when I remembered the scribbled-on pieces of paper inside.

You never left a note.

You never let us know why you chose to turn your insides into mush.

You never let us in to help you.

You never let me be enough to help save the two of us.

Brother,

There are so many I don't know where to begin. Some kind of look like they have numbers at the top of the page, like you were numbering your pain. But there is no order in the box. They are all thrown inside like they have been taken out and thrown away before.

There is an assortment of paper types, some colored, some lined, some in various half empty notebooks, some on the back of assignments. Some are written in pen, marker, crayon, pencil. You seem to have written on whatever you could get your hands on and kept them stashed in your pockets until you could hide them safely under my bed.

I keep opening it, shuffling the papers in the right order, and then tossing them back in the box.

I can't do it.

I don't want to know what drove you to kill yourself.

I don't want to know why you chose the escape of pills over life, over your little sister.

Did you not think of what kind of consequences your actions would have?

While you were running around burning bright and writing on whatever pieces of paper you could find, MaamaaBaabaa and I spoke in hushed voices of your change in character. The jingle of your pockets. I know I said I wouldn't, but I didn't promise to not tell them, just said "okay" when you told me not to tattle.

We made arrangements for you to get help. Prepared an intervention that did not happen as intended. They wanted to approach you and make you hopefully see a reason to get better before you turned eighteen and had control of whether you got help or not.

After I found you barely alive on that terrifying day, you let your systems run clean and came for a tour of the treatment center. We put our trust in you by returning home to wait and you came back one day blazing.

I wish we hadn't waited to admit you; maybe you would still be alive.

I have taken them all out and sorted them again.

I have stapled every ten pieces of paper and put a clip to hold them all in place. The scribblings in the notebooks were ripped out, but I figured the dead can't protest.

I have no excuse to not read them now.

I do not have to sit and agonize over finding the piece that comes next within the box of scribblings; I can pull the small stack of papers out of a pocket and read it whenever I want.

All that is lacking now is the motivation to put myself through the anguish.

Brother,

I have returned my things to the room and set everything to how it was before. Gathered snacks and drinks.

Ironically, it feels like when we would set up our room for a movie night. Instead of huddling over a small screen, I will find myself huddling over your scribblings, trying to make sense of the last year of your life.

Part II

if anyone ever asked,

 i said i wanted to be a poet.

 they replied that writing is hard.

believing entirely in the starving artist trope.

i wanted to say:

 living is hard, writing just makes it easier.

a pen was put in my hand
        and at the same moment
a brush was put into Andy's.

Maamaa chose me to be the writer,
Baabaa chose her to be the artist.

if they had chosen differently,
        would i feel differently?

the hardest part of writing:
    finding something to write about.
the popular choices are sex and love
but i've never been interested in those.

how can i want to be a writer,
        and not know what to write?
i could write about pain,
        but everyone does that.
my pain is nothing
        compared to what others experience.
i have nothing worth writing about
        and yet i have all these words bursting at my seams
                aching to be let out.

i dream of being a best-selling poet.
        my chapbook on the very first table of the commercial
            bookstores
        as well as the bookstore destined to be in my name.
i've been told to study English to improve my writing
but i do not want to do that.

writing is about experience and developing your own styles.
yes, they can guide you in schools
but i do not want that.
        i just want to be a poet.

i don't have a writing style.
i try to follow the shape of the stanzas from poets i find online.
i try to do longer poems but
i have trouble finding the attention span and reasons to write
    that way.
i want to have a writing style, or else
i might as well not be a poet.

Maamaa wanted me to be a writer.
she wanted to be a writer but ended up becoming
        a mother
        a shop owner.
i want to want to be a writer but i'm not the best writer.
i don't have reasons to write.
all i have is this
        emptiness inside that no one sees
that fills me with the urge to write but
        the pages
                stay
                        blank.

this emptiness has been with me for as long as Andy has.
it was as if as soon as she appeared
        a piece of me left.
she fills that shape that is emptied
but she cannot fill it forever.

feeling empty all the time is a peculiar feeling.
a happy glowing face is put on all day but behind the skin,
    everything is muted.
    everything is gray
    and lacks the warmth i pretend to radiate.
the emptiness is the closest thing i have to a lover
    and i want to break up.

alongside the emptiness comes along sadness.
    when the world slows down,
    the sadness moves in.

the world becomes even bleaker than before
and i feel catatonic.

in fact, i want to be catatonic.
it would be easier to sit there and succumb
to the feelings that have overcome my entire being.

i would rather feel
    the emptiness
    the sadness
and lose responsibilities than
pretend like i am fine every day.

every morning, i wake up to my mirror beside me
and put on a face that mimics hers.
i copy her light and put all my effort into being the outshining older brother.
i laugh
and talk
and hug
and hold
and talk
and talk.
it is easier to pretend to be happy than actually working to be happy.

it's really very easy to become happy.
if you have illness,
    you seek therapy and perhaps try medication alongside
        the therapy.
i don't have illness or past trauma to cause this constant feeling,
    therapy is out.

my parents believe illness is an imbalance within the spirit,
that i should move closer to my culture whenever i feel off.
    a culture that feels foreign.

therapy isn't a choice for me.
my only choice is to get close to
    a culture that was stolen from my lineage long ago.

my poetry isn't even poetry.
i write on the back of my assignments or scrap receipts that
customers do not want.
i vent and neglect to go back to my past writings to format
them properly.
i'm a lazy writer,
maybe i'm not meant to be a writer.

it was engraved in my life to be some type of artist.

    a creator of art.

Andy has her paints and art journals.

    it comes naturally to her.

writing doesn't come naturally to me.

    i want it to come naturally to me.

learning to write is harder than learning to be whole.

i try to be whole.
i do all the right things.
        socialize and
        meet new people and
        do the best i can.
but it is never enough.

the feeling of never being enough is a constant.
it's not a body image problem,
it's an identity problem.
i do not feel like i am enough for myself,
and thus,
i will never be enough for others.

my whole life is tied to my lack of identity.
i am born of this land since before contact
    but i have no culture
aside from a bit of language here and there
and the racial bias playing against me.
i am a technical twin
    but i have never lived as my own person.
i am a writer
    but i suck at it.
i have no identity,
no sense of self.

i am
born of this earth,
and yet,
i drown.

it feels like what other poets make a heartbreak sound like.
a disconnection from yourself
of something you once had.
but what if i
never had it before?

the best thing i can do for myself is talk about it
    and i honestly
        try.
i turn to my mirror
and prepare to tell her
        that her reflection is broken,
but i can't bring myself to do it.
i look into those deep black eyes
    and see myself looking back.
how do you tell your one constant
    that you feel like you are not alive?

i have taken to thinking to myself constantly.
i mutter to myself as i organize the shelves from Andy's latest
haul.
if i was ever alone,
i would talk aloud but i am never alone.
i don't think i would even begin to know how to be alone.

there is a part of me
that wishes
i was never
a part of
someone else.

i dream about a place of my own,
a place to call mine
        and only mine.
a small studio with the floor covered in stacks of books.
a few dying plants in the window.
this dream is unattainable.
i have never been on my own for more than a few hours,
    i could never live alone.
    i could never tell her
        i want my own space.

we are so entwined within each other that it feels as if we are the same person.
we are so identical it looks as if the twelve months between our births do not exist.
we are so enveloped within one another that we can never separate.

i have lived so long with a mirror beside me,
i don't know how to live without it.
i cannot begin to imagine a world without her.
a world in which we are not together.
i want a world in which we can coexist in our own lives while
remaining together.

i have tried to find my own path,
to divert from the urge to stain my fingers with ink
and stand proud with a metaphorical feather.
i have tried to be like the other kids,
to find the best quality brands at the charity shops and act like them.
i have tried to make myself small,
to hunch my shoulders and attempt to disappear.
i have tried to change the way my mind works,
to improve and become whole.
i have tried and i give up.

there are so many ways to change your brain chemistry.
    talk it out.
create to focus on anything else.
    pop a few to mimic the normal levels until you can on
        your own.

i cannot talk it out.
    i can't bring myself to tell my mirror that deep inside,
    my backing is cracked.
i try to create.
i write terrible poetry
    if it could even be called that.
i try to doodle but it turns into words.

i can't help but try to self-diagnose.
visiting a doctor for a psych evaluation is not an option for me.
i must do it myself.
there are so many disorders and long-term illnesses
and yet none seem to fit.

i have the compulsion
to become a person
that loses themselves in their self-care.
harmful or healing.
forget the world, their family.
focus on feeling better
in any way.

my parents do not drink.
    sometimes i wish they did.
i could steal a mouthful here and there,
    feel a buzz to forget the bees stinging my brain.
i have to deal with a swallowed splash of minty alcohol,
    an easy fuzz but not long-lasting.
green or gray smoke would be a better candidate,
    if my mirror would not sniff it out on our clothes.

occasionally a friend
will get a hold of burning liquid
and we spend the night feeling elated,
flying higher than we have in weeks.
i laugh without effort.
my voice amplified and musical.
the next day my face hurts from smiling so much.

my best friend is resourceful.
able to get most of what we want but
not everything is attainable.
no hard drugs or “drugs” in general.
but pharmaceuticals?
boxes of expired bottles and cabinets in walls.
easy to get.

i have done my research.
it takes a few days to weeks to kick in.
there are bottles hidden in the room,
    spaces my mirror would never check.

i wake up early and take it.
every day.

i am waiting for the day
that burst of energy comes and i begin to feel
in a way i never have before.

most days i feel so empty
i want to cry
but i am a well that has long ago dried up,
unable to find a water source.
i have guzzled liters upon liters of liquid to hydrate myself,
to prepare my body to exhaust that urge to cry feeling.
i try and try.
i watch sad videos,
i think of sad moments,
i think of the state of the world and the grim outlook of the future.
nothing works.
i could sit and stare at a wall all day and it would pass as quick as my good days.
some days i feel better.
my facial muscles begin to work again
and i am a light switch flicked on.
it's so repetitive.
back and forth.
bad and good.
i think there is no divide between the emotions.
the body feels alive one day and slowly
that energy drains out to nothing
and then it comes back again.
i have to coast to stay alive.

the meds definitely help but only so much.
the chemicals in the brain can be synthetically stimulated to
    have the hormones
it fails to produce but
that dimness on the inside still remains.

just because your head is lighter doesn't mean
that feeling is in your bloodstream,
racing to the rest of your body.

i should have expected it
to not be this easy.
life is never easy.
living is never easy.
finding a way to want to keep living is never easy.
it would be easier to succumb to this lack of light within myself.

i stare at my mirror so intently sometimes
 i think she will crack.
she does in my imagination sometimes.
this deafening sound blocks out all sound waves from hitting
 my eardrums
 and i am left staring at my mirror.
i want to let the dam burst.
i urge a crack in the foundation to appear.
 tell her tell her
 tell her tell her
that her mirror is cracked and needs help.

i've run out.
i didn't think much about what would happen when i did.
my hopes got the better of me
and i thought i could keep a steady supply for myself,
that he could always get what i need.
the meds were old,
half-empty things found rattling in the back of drawers and
    cabinets.
if i hadn't doubled the dose to get quicker results,
wasn't scared of ineffectiveness with age,
i would've had more time to find another source.
maybe if it lasted until i turned eighteen
i could have gotten my own.

the emptiness is creeping back again.
a reminder that no matter what i try,
it will always swallow me.

it comes slowly,
like the sun leaving the sky.
the light is just past the horizon,
but in front of it is darkness.
shaded trees and dimmed buildings,
spaces of brightness instead but not forever.
before long, the sun is merely a memory
and it feels as if this darkness is here to stay.

i feel most like myself
        when i cannot feel myself.
i feel like i have my own self
        when i am not myself.
i feel as if i have my own singular identity
        when i cannot recognize my reflection.

everything is so carefully hidden.
the last traces of pharmaceuticals bought off
the girl with a sleek ponytail, packed into old shoes.
tinned wrappers taped to the bed stand.
uppers and downers in opposite directions.
my own induced paradise hidden throughout my life
to hide my emptiness from the sunshine.

i wish i was Buddhist or Sikh or Muslim or Jewish.
i wish i had a religion that i belonged to.

somewhere i am entirely accepted.
somewhere a Creator loves me faults and all.

i need faith to understand why i came into this world alone
and why
i feel that loneliness down to my core.

if i could lose myself in other people
i would.
        a mess of warm skin and gasps and fluids.
        a smile and a blessed thank-you for my charity.
if i could completely lose myself and be reborn,
i would.

i spent my entire life
being a part of someone else
when all i needed
was to be myself.

that's the thing about never being yourself:
you don't know how to *be.*
simply *being* is too much to bear.

taking up space and
allowing yourself to try new things and
finding yourself is never an option.

your existence is not your own and
it never will be.

when starting over
becomes too difficult
to achieve,
ruining every chance
becomes an easier path.

i am falling in love

    and it is scaring the last bits of living out of me.

i always thought i would fall for a person with

    warm skin and a bright smile,

not any substance i can get my hands on for a reasonable price.

wake up
feel the burn down your throat
pop a mint and whatever the white pill is
go about your day.

behave as if
you are another human being
on the same level of consciousness as everyone else.

come home
pop the other yellowed pills
and ride the high into the sunset.

it has become a routine,
and after all,
isn't that what humans need most?
a reason to get up
and attempt to live each day,
a reason to continue the life no one asked for.

i would like to say i've never been suicidal,
that even with this overbearing humidity clouding my senses
and the darkness inside

i have never thought about taking my own life.

there's a truth and a lie to that statement.
i have thought about dying prematurely
but not about intentionally doing it.

i wouldn't tie my own noose
but i wouldn't look twice walking across the expressway.

there are times when i think people have caught on.
    Andy, my ever-faithful mirror,
has begun reflecting my new behaviors.
i can tell she does not understand where
this new personality has come from but
    enjoys it too much to ask.
she wouldn't enjoy it if
she knew what i hide under her bed.

one day we stumble off the bus
and she grips my hand so hard
my bones would break if i could feel them,

drags me up the stairs and into
the empty apartment.
tell me what is wrong with you. you aren't right, let me help you.

i try to laugh it off and say
she is making something out of nothing.

she set it up so well,
arranged the room to resemble when we were kids.
she grabs one of my ever-tattered books
and sits across the beds,
patting the space next to her.
i am unable to stop myself and i snuggle into her side
while my little sister reads to me and strokes my hair.

she is trying.
she is trying to find out what is wrong.

asking where i got it from.
asking why.

i say there is no end.
i say there was never a beginning,
        just the inevitable.

it is said over and over
by multiple misunderstood people
but here it goes:

no one knows me.
my own sister doesn't know me.
i don't know me.

how am i supposed to even think about ever "getting better"
if i don't want what i am supposed to go back to.

in my daydreams,
i am a person with a strong posture and an air of inner security.
i am a person who knows who they are and to whom they
belong.

in these passing moments,
i can see a different life for us.

i am Alexander and without fear.
i am Alexander and no one else.

they sit you down
and say this is not an intervention.
    we are just worried.
    you're different and it's scaring us.
of course, i'm different.
i couldn't live in the person i was before
and this is preferable to death.

the shadow of a child in my memories wants to accuse her of
lying to me.
i told her not to tell but she never said the magic words.
all she wants is her brother back
but she never had me in the first place.

once upon a time … there was a son,
waiting eagerly in the brightly lit sterile hallway,
bopping on an anxious knee of the neighbor.
she is humming to herself
and i am listening to the room i was not allowed in.
i feel the shock before i hear the wail of new life
and i am no longer only a son,
but a brother.

a part of me wants to let them make me better.
another part of me wants to fight tooth and nail,
to stay with the path i am on.

we push our beds together like when we were little.
in the darkness she feels for my hand and gives it a soft squeeze.
if you're not ready that's okay. i'll always be here for you
when you are.
i bite my lip until there is blood staining my teeth,
but my body is so high that i barely felt her next to me.
i don't think i'll ever be ready.

my mirror does what she can.
she has taken up the job of reading aloud before bed every
    night like that first night,
scouting the city's yard sales for addiction memoirs and resting
    my head in her lap
while i try to come down enough to hear her voice.

i like being taken care of.
she checks up on me,
apologizes for staying quiet before,
apologizes for telling Baabaa.
everyone is so happy to see me acting the way i used to.
it all feels so fake.

surprisingly, my grades are better than before.
i take too much before testing
and don't remember my answers
but my report card says i'm doing well.
i send applications for different programs,
for college,
for university.
the world is at my fingertips as long as i have my stash.

life is moving
and the world is in my reach
and yet i feel more lost than ever.
i do not even know who I am
as a singular person.
how am I meant to choose my future?

in my dreams,
we found who we are
        and i leave.

i return to the place our ancestors were assigned to.
flying home in a rusty car,
        groaning down the dusty roads.

i often say *see you again*
and drive away to the next city for work,
        always returning home.

the emptiness is an absence.
an absence of self.
and the emptiness expands
the more i try to fill it
in all the wrong ways.

occasionally i take too much.
my brain is so muddled that i cannot comprehend anything
and it takes a long time before
i fly down enough to return to my consciousness.

i am drying up.
my last lifeline refuses to get me more,
to get me anything.

the one who gave to me at first
says i need to listen to Andy and get help.

in the before,
i went to him for help and he gave me pills.

eventually,
my habits become another mode of life for us.
i see the sadness in everyone's eyes but for once i don't see it in mine.
they want me to get clean but why
would i do that if i would go back to how i was before.

getting better would be harder than getting high.
i can't just stop and
go back to the emptiness within my bones.
i would need professional help to address the space and
i don't think i'm ready for that.
i'd rather lie and
say i am going to quit than crack my head open and
let them probe me.

she scratched my throat with her fingernails.
the pain in my throat feels the same as the pain in my being.
it hurts more than my pounding head and aching sweats.

my mirror looks so terrible.
she is the embodiment of how my insides feel.
tangled hair and blotched face.
her light burning so dim it feels as if
her candle is almost out.

i convinced the doctor to release me.
the withdrawal is over and
it would take a while until a spot is open for me at the
    treatment center,
which means i have a while more to feel the way i love.

they didn't think to go through our room.
the trust they have in me is astounding.
you don't believe an addict will resist their hiding places
just because the substances are out of their system.

i am back into my habits
but my parents ignore it for now.
i have a spot waiting for me after the holidays.
but i have not run dry.

my mirror wants to believe that
i am getting better so deeply that she believes i have.
warm smiles and a praise for battling my addiction
as if the image she has of me in her mind is true.

i am fairly sure that i need a higher dosage now.
taking too much that one day
means my tolerance is higher now.
i don't feel as elated as i used to.

my ex–best friend thinks he knows me,
thinks he can see through my lies and tell me what to do.
he's the one that got me this way.
he doesn't see me telling him not to touch my sister.
he can't act all high and mighty when he's a hypocrite.

i don't have friends anymore.
i have become Andy's shadow until the school year is over.
i am still a delight to be around
but Krish won't look me in the eye anymore.

my habits were not left behind in the hospital bed.
they were not washed away with the sheets.

my habits have become habits.
no longer are they for coping,

i need them to feel alive more than i ever have,
more than Andy ever has.

it is my daily routine now.
how could i ever think of leaving them behind?

recovery is a possibility.
i would like to be an actual person.
without the help of substances
it could be a better life for me than what i have currently
but it feels so far away.

the problem with having a problem
is that you might acknowledge that you have a problem
but you don't want to live without the problem
because you need to address the problem to get rid of it.

it is a tug of war.
i want to be better.
they want me to be better.
but somewhere in the middle, i don't know how.
i don't know how to get better,
        how to be better,
                how to take the steps i need to be a whole person.

there are days when i go without.
those days i think
yes, i can get better i can get sober i can become a real person i can be better
and then that emptiness crashes back in
and i find myself fighting to reset my sobriety tracker.

as a child we were brought to the woods and sent out to play.
we ran and ran
giggling
and fumbling over growing legs
and the wind tangling our hair
hiding in the exposed roots of the Mother
jumping into trees and being as quiet as possible.
i feel as alive with my stomach acid degrading drugs as i did back then.

i never thought i would be this person.
you think of addicts, and you think what you were told to
believe.
you think they are people that do this to themselves
and need to do the work themselves
or they don't deserve to function in our society.
or at least that's what i thought until i realized
i became one.

the first step is acceptance, right?
stand up tall and say:
    my name is Alexander and I am an addict.
pretend you are content being in a room full of other addicts
  trying to recover
when the reality is that
you want to be with the ones that relapse.

the center seems nice.
they tell me they can help me
emotionally
physically
spiritually.

to think that i could possibly find my culture
in a place that i have to detox in,
is making recovery seem appealing.

a little lie i like to tell myself:
if our room wasn't full of my goodies
maybe i could have stayed sober.

another lie is that i am ready to make this big change.
it took a matter of weeks for me to become an addict,
could a few weeks in a naturally lit building make me sober?
there is a long road ahead and
i am not sure if i am strong enough to take it.

the date is coming quick and
i have so much more hidden away than i could ever have
thought.
this will not do.
it needs to be gone.

i was raised to finish my plate
fix tattered clothing
waste not want not and all that.
how could i possibly throw away my lifelines
in such a wasteful way as opposed to using them one last time.

Part III

Once upon a time, two children lived in the world hand in hand with dreams and aspirations but without courage. The brother held up his sister so she could walk, and eventually, the sister tried to hold up her brother so he could run. She failed, again and again, until finally the world won.

The sister watched in despair as her mirror broke more by the day. There was so much she wanted to do to help but so little time. The brother was falling fast and could not find the will to survive.

One day, he chose to heal. But healing did not choose him.

I devoured your scribblings before the city's skyline began to lighten with the early sun. Originally, I had thought to take my time and read pieces as I felt prepared for it, but I am glad I decided against that and went headfirst into the shoebox.

The funny thing is, I felt numb while I read your poetry. I could see the rise and falls of your short-lived addiction with each piece. It brought back a lot of memories, and I began to feel as hollow as I felt before I started college. The way I had seen it, the hole I felt inside all my life was a backsplash. As long as I had you, it was manageable. I could fill the emptiness with *nisaye* and feel better as long as I could see my reflection in identical eyes.

After you took the rest of your "stash" and didn't wake up, the emptiness ravaged my body, and I was sleepwalking.

Is that how you felt all the time?

As if you were an outline of a person on autopilot?

Was I not enough for you?

In a different reality, I would have been.

Some days I stare into space and imagine what our opposite realities must be doing. You would have gone to some far-off school with the program that interested you the most and perhaps would have encouraged me to do the same. But the emptiness would have remained until we developed enough courage to deal with it.

I thought I had gotten that courage. It made sense to me: if having someone else complete me took the edge off, then why wouldn't it work again? However, people are unpredictable. Helena is aromantic and could never love me back. You killed yourself because *you didn't want to be wasteful.* I have come to realize that I am never enough for others but maybe all I really need is to be enough for myself.

It is a complex concept. *Being enough.* Everyone has different ideas of "good enough," but does anyone fit those definitions?

I had never given much thought to what my definition could be. In fact I had automatically thought that I was enough until proven wrong.

The dead cannot speak, and yet I feel as if I failed as a *shiimen*. Having *nisaye* was plenty for me. You were all I needed to tether me to this world. It wasn't until I began to notice the difference in you that I began to think that I was wrong.

Maybe the problem was not me. Maybe nothing would have been enough for you. You had the love and adoration of those near and dear to you. Still, it is clear that you ached for more.

As children we would huddle under the blankets and spin tales of what our future would be like. You wanted to go on an adventure of discovery and find where all your puzzle pieces fit. I was content to follow the life plan laid out for me. Should I have encouraged you more?

Maybe I should have promised to go with you.

Dear Brother,

I cannot help but blame myself.

I let it go on for so long, standing off to the side and witnessing your downfall. The thoughts of what I could have done (what I should have done) run through my head constantly. I try to listen to my college lectures and customers, but I am preoccupied with the dead.

You are constantly on my mind. The shape of your face, the curve of your smile, the emptiness in your eyes that I never noticed while you were alive. You were more than my twin. You were my older brother, a son, a friend.

You were a person, an individual, and you were in pain.

The pain consumed you. Burning away everything you could have been. The consumption grew to be so great that you needed to consume other things to blunt the edges. The pain and emptiness sound so abstract but I have felt them too. I knew how you felt; why didn't you confide in me? We could have helped each other.

Dear Brother,

When I stop and allow myself to feel, when I explore the hollows of my being, I can imagine doing the same.

In the moments that I allow myself to rest, to stop occupying myself with tasks, I begin to feel like an outline. There is nothing inside. I am a hollow shell and I ache to be full. I get the urge to be filled and I find the kitchen empty after I snap back to reality.

It would not have been hard to fall into substances. When the assignments and the homework and the studying are done and I don't have a shift or friends to see, I would welcome a way to not feel like myself. Having nothing to do is the only time I begin to feel, and I do everything in my ability to avoid it.

Rather than falling into the arms of pills and drink, I fell into the arms of others. It is mechanical and easy to focus on motions and people. Now that I am without a person to use, I realize how I am no different from you. You had used substances to feel different; I used people. I trapped Helena in a fantasy of what I believed I needed. I allowed Krish to believe there was something being formed while I had no interests other than my own. I was not a good person to others, and you were not a good person to yourself.

After the door was locked and we awaited professional cleaning, I sat with my back against the opposite wall for days. Staring at our growth marks on the door. I thought a lot about promises. The promises I should have made. The little promises I had the time to make. The promises you made and broke. All of the pinky swears and whispers, broken and forgotten in the wind.

We had promised to always be there for each other.

I tried to keep my end of the bargain. By gods did I try.

I surveyed your moods, tried to replicate them so no one would notice. I believed that I alone could help. As usual, I was wrong.

However, I believe I did everything I could. Everything I could manage.

There is so much more that I could have done but it is far too late now. I can sit on this bus and write as much as I want, I can stare off into the distance seeing nothing and everything, and still, nothing can bring you back. Nothing will be the same again and I have to reconcile with the fact that I was not enough to save you from yourself.

I never realized how much of a people pleaser I am, how much I want to be accepted and loved and make everyone's boo-boos go away.

After you died, I tried to lift MaamaaBaabaa's spirits. I made Baabaa's favorite meals from childhood but could never get the recipe right, or when I did, my efforts would make no difference. I am always trying to fix others. Trying to make everyone feel all right so that I may feel better about myself.

I have always lost myself in the problems of others. In school I was the go-to friend to vent to, the person you dump your emotions on, all the while masquerading that I was fine. I was so lost and disconnected that I never took the time to evaluate my own emotions rather than analyzing everyone else's. It feels wrong to think about myself. It makes me feel selfish, but no matter how uncomfortable it makes me feel, I have to learn to prioritize myself.

Dear Brother,

I know I need to change for the better, but I am afraid. This is all I know, and I am not ready to start on a new path. Trying to accept the fact that life changes again and again is suffocating.

I want things to be the way they were before, or rather the way they appeared.

I want a brother by my side, and I want to feel whole. I want the charade we displayed to be a reality.

In my downtime during shifts I leaf through self-help books. They encourage acknowledging that things need to change for the better and making those changes. I can read every book in that section and still I am lost at what I must do. I can acquire every bit of knowledge I can regarding my current problem, but I lack the resources to do something about it.

Truthfully, I lack the courage to do something about it.

I've tried talking to Baabaa about this.

It has always been easier for me to be vulnerable with our father. I know he doesn't have as high expectations of me as Maamaa does.

He calls me *daanis* and tries to say that it is okay, that I am young and have plenty of time to figure myself out. I want to scream and yell that no matter how many times he says that it does not feel true. I need to be grown *now.* I need to be strong *now.* I need to be emotionally intelligent *now.*

Things come crashing down and I am hyperventilating, trying to force air into my body but my body rejects it. I try and try, and it is never enough. I am not even enough for my own body; how could I have ever thought I would be enough for anyone else?

I want to be fixed and I want it now. I want all my cracks to be glued back together. I want my life before but better. I want you next to me always and I want independence from our constant codependency.

There are so many things I want but no way to achieve them. I cannot bring back the dead and your resurrection would not fix me. I know that I know that I know that I know that but that does not stop the aching emptiness in my chest.

I want to be fixed but I do not know how to fix myself.

You see, Brother,

I had never put much thought into how I could properly fix myself for good before things changed. I was quite content with my life while you were still in it. Sure, I didn't have Delilah and James, or Helena for that matter, but I was content with you and Krish by my side. He and I would not have lasted, I know that. But I would have enjoyed life as long as I had both of you with me.

I was able to pretend that things were swell and ignore the inching ache that threatened to consume me. As long as I refused to acknowledge it, I was fine, and now that I am allowing myself to be aware of the gap in my chest where I would otherwise feel a tightness, I feel so helpless.

As far as I was concerned, I did not need to be fixed because there was nothing coming to my immediate attention that needed to be addressed. Now that I am allowing myself to acknowledge it, it is all I can think about.

It is consuming me.

If it is possible that there is anything left to consume.

It is funny in a way how much I had wanted the consumption of love. I wanted to relish in the feeling of my veins set afire, the so-called love racing around my body to keep me warm. I wanted Helena to love me so badly that I thought she did.

Deep down, I was convinced that I was a damsel who needed to be saved for life to feel complete. I wanted a love to function as butane dripped onto my candle and it became a raging bonfire within. I was convinced that I would be a phoenix rising from the ashes. I wanted the fire to burn away the outline of myself and I would be reborn from the ashes mixing with the earth.

Everything I did, everything I thought, was wrong. I thought I needed another person. I thought I needed love. I thought I could help you. I was so wrong, and it feels like there is nothing I can do about it.

What I truly needed was someone to convince me that the feelings and dealings of others were not on my shoulders. It was not my job in life to be in charge of that; it was never assigned to me.

I should have been concerned about myself. I should have been focused on building a sense of self rather than building everyone up with the pieces of my being.

Ally, I'm sorry but

I'm honestly surprised you knew.

We thought we were being secretive because it was something that just happened. Krish had harbored feelings toward me for a while by the first time he kissed me, but I never felt the same way. It was nice to be loved for a while and he was a good distraction from the grief, but it would have never become anything unless I found myself content enough to marry him in the future. I didn't want him to hold on to me while he was away for school and told him as much, but truthfully, I do not think I could have brought myself to love him as more than a friend.

(Wow, and here I was judging Helena for a similar situation.)

Anyway, it is nice to finally admit it. There were times I wanted to tell you, but I was afraid of how you would react. Now, I'm glad I ended it. Even though he had stopped supplying you eventually, it doesn't change the fact that he was the first one to give you what you thought you needed. Due to our history, I believe I will always see him as a close friend and (almost) family, but I do not think I could look him in the eye now that I know the secrets he had hidden from me.

We both loved him, and he loved us, but somewhere along the way things began to go wrong. I have come to accept that everything will not stay the same as life goes on. Childhood friends may be left behind in childhood memories and it is a surface-level grief. It is about acceptance more than loss.

I have accepted that a vital relationship in my childhood grew into an unsustainable secret built on differing needs. Krish and I always had an unsaid expiration date of graduation. He is now an old friend that may one day fade into a memory.

Lately, I have been thinking about what your life would have been like if I had never existed. If the mistake child had never happened. I had felt like that before, the overwhelming urge to not exist. You would have had your own room, your own friends, more shifts at the shop, a different life experience.

The lack of self would not have been an issue for you if I never existed. There would have been identity issues no doubt — we never got to embrace our indigeneity because our parents didn't know how. If I had not existed, would you have been more drawn to discovering our culture and healing yourself that way?

The truth is, I can ask paper and pen as much as I want and will never get the answers to my questions. I do not wish to leave our parents with no children at all just because I wish that you still existed on the physical plane and that I never did on the chance you may have felt better on the inside.

The only thing I can do is move forward. Set simple short- and long-term goals (fix my crumbling friendships and graduate college) and live each day because you are not able to anymore. Maybe if I make my life mean something, if I stop coasting through life, it will honor the life you lost.

There are so many possibilities out there in the world and the sad thing is, I know nothing of what I want. I do not know myself; I spent a lifetime being part of a shared identity and I do not know who I am as my own person.

Sometimes I catch myself and realize this or that is something I like, something I enjoy, something I want. I make lists in my head: I enjoy heavily spiced food, sci-fi disaster movies, the crackling feeling of paint on my fingers, laughing so hard with friends that we forget how to breathe, the small smile on a customer's face when they find a book they have been searching for, playing the radio and dancing in the kitchen with our parents.

I want to be whole. I want to discover who I am, and I pray to whatever gods will listen that I will become someone worthwhile.

The knowledge that I tried to destroy my friendships as fast as I made them was gnawing at my ribs and I left my shift early in an attempt to catch the bus before the routes ended for the night. I ran in the early December air and felt disappointment in my chest when I saw the bus drive away, but the disappointment quickly disappeared after the tiny burst of energy from running filled my veins. Their apartment isn't very far away on foot and so I ran.

I haven't properly run since early high school, and I stumbled in your boots. What a sight I must have been. A flash of long dark hair in the night, dodging dog walkers and cars, trying not to slide on the ice and snow. I arrived at their door breathing heavier than I ever had in my life but feeling more elated than I ever have.

James answered the door and was taken aback by the slowly frostbitten, out of breath, grinning person standing on his doorstep. He explained that Delilah was out and began to close the door. I felt a stab of pain that I had centered myself around Delilah and Helena so much that James and I were simply acquaintances that enjoyed the same movies. I insisted that I would like to see him too, that he is also my friend if he will have me.

He turned the kettle on and wrapped a blanket around my shoulders. "Why are you here?" he asked. "I thought you were mad at us."

I was and I shouldn't have been. None of this was any of your fault and it was wrong of me to get so angry. I miss you and Delilah and Helena, and I wish things were back the way they were when things were simpler.

"Things are never simple, and they rarely go back to the way you want them."

I understand that now. It's just that I have never had my own friends, my own life. I'm not very good at any of it and I just want everything to be better. I want to be a better friend.

"You always were a good friend, Andria. And besides, who is good at life? The point of life is making it good for yourself, not changing to be good for others."

I'm glad you're my friend, James. I mean, if you're still my friend.

And then he smiled that smile that makes me feel like everything will be better, and for that moment in time, it was.

We stayed up and spent the time talking at their little kitchen table. Now that I try to think back on it, I don't remember much of what we talked about, but I do know that I had a good time. Even Maamaa's anger when I got home the next early morning wasn't enough to dull the brightness of my candle.

She raged on for a while about how dangerous it is for us to walk in the city, especially at night and alone. Had I not remembered the numerous articles, the news reports, or the novels written about the dangers of our city? Did I want to become a statistic that continued growing despite political promises? I let her rage on, and when she was done and started to get mad because I was smiling at her, I hugged her.

A sad thing to admit is that I do not remember the last time I hugged our mother before that. I'd spent so long thinking of myself and trying to understand the dead, I had forgotten that while I had lost a brother, she had lost a son and somehow along the way had lost a daughter in the process.

We stood there for so long embracing each other that her hair began to wet from the tears that found their way out of my eyes and Baabaa was surprised to find us in the kitchen with no coffee on. He joined in and the hug continued. Eventually we slid onto the floor and cried while we held on to each other. (In an odd way, it reminded me of the group bear hugs that squished the giggles out of us as children.)

I had spent so long focused on my own grief that I had not acknowledged the grief they held. Maybe that makes me a bad daughter, but I intend to be the best daughter I can from now on. I told them as such and MaamaaBaabaa wiped away my tears, telling me that I am their daughter and that is enough for them.

Too much of my life was spent going with the flow. Especially this year, this semester. I was given so many opportunities so quickly that I never actually took the time to focus entirely on them.

Take my volunteering, for example. I truly have no idea how Maamaa managed to get me the gig. Now that I think about it, I think you need a degree at least for what I have been doing. On second thought, they're more workshops than art therapy, so maybe it's okay. Regardless, I have realized how much I enjoy the classes.

After we had finally gotten up off the kitchen floor, I showered and was off to the center. I took my time greeting each patient and tried to make the class more helpful to their recovery than I have been the past few months.

Close your eyes and let your mind go blank. Listen to my voice. What do you want out of life? Sketch the first image that came into your thoughts.

I milled around the room and, for the first time, truly saw the talent and people of the room. There was a clear theme to the pieces: happiness.

Everyone's happiness is different. I asked some of the patients what their pieces were to get a better idea of who they are. A lot of the answers were "my family" or "go back to school" or "learn xyz."

One piece in particular stood out to me. I had complimented the man's work before; his style was beautiful and reminded me a lot of what you see in the art museum on campus and around the city in general. This piece was complex and zoomed in; I had difficulty recognizing what it was and so I asked.

He gave me a shy smile and said, "I'm surprised you don't recognize it. These are pieces of the regalia from my childhood.

I felt so happy dancing for others. When I get out of here and maintain my sobriety, I want to dance again."

We had never gone to ceremony and the only time I had seen it was online. His piece was so beautiful that I almost asked for it but thought better of it.

Do you remember the day after we both turned ten and Maamaa sat us down at the kitchen table? With tears swimming behind her eyes, she held Baabaa's hand and told us the story of her life.

She had no original identity of her own. Taken from her parents at birth in the hospital and shuffled from home to home. For eighteen years she was forced to move around multiple foster homes, hoping that one day someone would be captivated with her enough to adopt her. That day never came, and instead, she aged out of the system. No family, no idea of her roots, her reserve. She was born in a city in another province but doubted that her parents lived there. Luckily, she had met Baabaa by the time she was thrown out on her own.

Baabaa clutched her hand so tightly I thought her skin was going to split. A faraway look overcame Maamaa's eyes as it sometimes did and Baabaa took his turn.

He told us that he grew up with his parents but often felt as if it would have been better if he hadn't. You see, our grandparents had been stolen away and forced into a world that never felt right. They were young enough that being scooped did not make sense to them until they realized there was no way to go back to a home they had long forgotten by the time they returned to the earth.

They fully took on the Catholic life in place of their stripped culture and Baabaa was never given the opportunity to learn his heritage, his culture. All he learned was how to hide when the bottles were purchased. He told us in a raspy voice that he does not blame every Catholic he encounters for what happened. Some days he felt there could be so many fingers pointed that he stopped the blaming game. All that mattered was breaking the cycle.

MaamaaBaabaa met in the city five years before we were born in it, and as soon as the tests came back positive, they promised each other to provide different lives for us than the ones they had.

Baabaa told us to learn our culture through school and listen closely when we find new information. We were given different lives than the ones they endured, and it was our duty to find ourselves as we were meant to be.

Now that I think of this core memory and remember how we cried in bed together after, how we promised each other we would do what our parents wanted of us, I am not sure how to feel. We were ten years old and did not know what our teen years would bring. We wanted to snap our fingers and be exactly what MaamaaBaabaa wanted us to be: a continuation of culture. Now that I think of it, that was a heavy burden to place upon children.

Dear Ally,

It probably is not the best thing in the world to do, but I have been rereading your poems.

Going over your poems is jarring, to say the least. I can pinpoint what stages you were at by how much or how little you wrote, what you wrote about. Each time, I half expect to finally find your suicide note.

That's what it was listed as: Suicide by Overdose.

The idea had never sat well with me. There was no way you would willingly kill yourself, not without telling me you had thought of ending your life as a way to get help faster. The doctors had even listed your first overdose as a suicide attempt, but I found your drugs and told Baabaa.

That's why MaamaaBaabaa knew how to get you into the addictions program.

It is almost comforting to know that you weren't trying to kill yourself, you were trying to kill that piece of you that was forever missing. I didn't fill that space; in fact, I still think I made it worse. You took the rest to not be wasteful and to keep yourself from relapsing after you got released from the hospital. There's no other explanation that makes sense and you stated it exactly: you didn't want to be wasteful, and it killed you.

I noticed right away when you started to get bad, even before the pills came into play. You kept saying that you were fine, and nothing was wrong, but I saw the way you dimmed. And then your flame shot through the ceiling once you went to the illegal stuff. It became exhausting to replicate, especially since I knew it was temporary and hurting you. I should have done more — taken the pills from you, made you stop. I felt so helpless watching my big brother burn too bright. I had the constant sickening feeling that you were going to be snuffed out and I was too late when I felt your fire disappear.

I wish I had done something before it got bad. Things for me are slowly getting better but I believe that I will carry this guilt for the rest of my life. If I had done something earlier, would you be alive?

So many times, I have wished that I told you that I felt that emptiness too. I tried to lose myself in being your twin over losing myself to the emptiness, and later, I tried to lose myself in Krish. I feel so vile knowing I was sleeping with the person that got you on drugs. I scrubbed my skin until it hurt in the shower each time after reading those poems.

Do you think you would be alive if we were more truthful with each other? I think so. You could have gotten proper therapy and learned how to cope in healthy ways. As for me, I don't think I would have made the mess of my life that I have.

It is almost pathetic to think of it now. I finally got my own friends and a girlfriend, and I burned it all to the ground out of what I thought was rejection. Those people loved me. Maybe not all in the same way I loved them, but still, they loved me.

I have confidence that James forgives me and still believes in me as a friend, but I still need to make more amends for what I've done. There is no point in wishing I could change what happened in the past when I can repair what I have done in the present. I need to talk to Delilah and Helena.

Especially Helena. I now know a little bit of what it must be like from her point of view, and I want to patch things up as best as I can.

I half expected her to never speak to me again. I called during one of her classes when I knew she would have her phone off and she called as soon as the class was done. I felt like a broken record with my constant apologizing, but she was patient as always. I spent the phone call begging and trying to make up for how terrible I had been, and she kept silent, letting me get it out of my system.

After I had finally run out of energy and words, all she said was "Where do you live? I'm coming over."

She pulled up in her little compact and I gave her a brief tour of the shop. Maamaa was a little bit taken aback but warmed up after the introductions and suggested I take Delilah with me in search of the next inventory.

There is something intimate about looking for books together. She was excited to do the shopping with me and I was just excited to have my friend back. Delilah explained that I never actually lost her, just that she was patiently waiting until I was back to myself after getting my heart broken.

I tried to focus on the present and just us in that moment.

Being in the car with Delilah felt so right. Every time my breath began to hitch, and I found myself overthinking, she would smile, and I would be centered again. We drove around the city, checking out the very few garage sales and filling the car with boxes of books. The radio was on and Delilah loves singing so there was no pressure to talk.

I felt lighter than I have in days. If I have Delilah back, I can do anything.

Oh, Brother Dearest,

I wish you could meet Delilah. I think you would have loved her as much as I do just from meeting her once.

I slipped up when we were laughing, and the laughter began to die down.

My brother would have loved you.

She looked like I had grabbed her arm after dragging my socks on a carpet.

"Brother?"

Yeah. I had a brother.

I made sure not to mess up my tenses this time and she caught on immediately. Her face softened and her eyes felt like they burned.

"Tell me about him."

At first, I felt defensive that she was demanding rather than asking, but before I knew it, words and stories and our life began pouring out of my body so quickly I was barely able to register it.

I told her about how we were one person in two bodies that looked identical and about how we were always there for each other until we couldn't be. I told her about the time we tried climbing on top of the building and almost met the pavement before we met the sky. She listened so patiently to all my stories that I hardly noticed when she pulled into a park, and I let a lifetime pour out of me onto the windshield.

It felt good to tell someone else. To be able to talk about it. I even told her about your last few months and the scribblings and how I found them and how the emptiness ate us both alive, but I was the only one left breathing. At some point she took my hand and I talked and talked until my phone started buzzing with Maamaa asking where I was.

We went back home and unloaded the car while Baabaa told us where to put the boxes. He didn't blink twice at Delilah and invited her up for dinner. It wasn't an elaborate meal, but she drank in everything about the apartment. At some point we wandered into the room, and she started listing off ideas of how to make it mine when I was ready. She looked through our things with my permission and found the bag gathering dust in the back of the closet.

"Maybe these can help," she said while holding up a brush.

It is muscle memory at this point.

I lay out the brushes, the paints, the pencils, the paper, the panel. I flip through my old catalogs of art in the form of diaries as I sit on the floor. Grab a glass and fill it with water, grab the newspapers and a cloth. Arrange everything just so. My fingers twitch for the feeling of dried paint under my nails. A memory of burning back muscles.

And yet I cannot think. I used to grab a brush and pick paints and start without too much thought into it.

Used to.

At some point during the time when I was trying to forget the emptiness that you once filled, I had also forgotten my passion. I cannot remember how to mix the colors. I cannot remember which brush is for each stroke.

I am a body of forgotten memories and lost hands.

I sat and stared for so long that the daylight disappeared. I vaguely remember how I did it before but the brush that used to be the extension of my arm now feels unfamiliar. It feels heavy and wrong.

My previous pieces are scattered on the floor. Some completed, some half finished, some barely started, some needing something else to make it *right.*

We step around the hobby on the living room floor and pretend to not notice that I have forgotten how to use a brush. Maamaa smiles because she knows that although I have yet to create something, I am trying.

I am sitting and staring, and, on the inside, I am crying but I am trying.

I am trying and maybe that is all that matters.

The wind is getting colder, and the world is muffled with snow and clouded skies. The world is silent and eerie in the dawn.

I have taken to sleeping as soon as school and work are over if I am home and waking up before dawn's rosy fingers touch the sky.

Somewhere out there in the cold is Helena. She is running along the campus, cheeks wind chapped and hair frosted. I cannot see her from my window, but I know she is out there.

She ran for pleasure and as a way to pass the time. I ran away from everything dear to me.

On these mornings, I think about what could have been and I wish she would run to me. Her chest raising and falling, trying to warm the air with her lungs. Our hands held and fingers running through my hair.

It is not meant to be and really what is? Life changes so rapidly without warning that I cannot allow myself to fixate on how I want my life to be, on how much I want things to be the way I feel most content. Some things are not meant to be and that is simply fine.

Ally,

Maybe, you and I were not meant to be.

We were not meant to be twins. We were not meant to be a singular entity.

Maybe, only one of us was ever meant to exist. The doctors said that none of us would and yet we did for a fleeting time.

Things would have been different if our births were not in the same year or if we did not look like copies of each other. We could have been siblings, not a singular unit, and led parallel lives, not tangled threads.

Everything feels like a big what-if and I imagine those thoughts will simply be a part of my life now. A low whisper whenever I think of you.

Dear Brother,

For so long I was filled with despair and anger over your death. You were so young, and it wasn't fair that your life ended so quickly. Slowly, things have been changing for me and the biggest change is my perspective.

In a terrible way, I am glad it was quick. Your decline and addiction started fast and ended fast. The grief I was consumed by and continue to feel would've been a waking existence if you had lived.

Over time I am sure that you would have started trying more and more until you found exactly what made you feel alive. All the while, MaamaaBaabaa and I would have been forced to watch you become a walking death. You could have run away, and I would have started spending my time trying to bring you home, trying to get you clean.

Your death was a clean break from the pain that could have been, and I have grown to accept it.

Everything is simpler than my collapsing lungs would lead me to believe.

I can enter their home and she is there on the couch ripping at their magazines. A welcoming smile and unsaid forgiveness. An agonizing apology and a dismissive hand.

"It happens. I am glad you are working past it," she says and flips the next page.

We fall into a room, a house, of love that I had previously misinterpreted. Four friends lay on top of each other, bickering over movies and whether we want to try a new culinary creation or order out.

It is possible for the pieces to fall in place without forcing the corners to fit. It hurts less to let go of the rough rope as it shreds away the last of your palms than it does to treat it as your lifeline.

I have been putting so much of an emphasis on everything going wrong that I made it all out to be harder than it truly was.

I got Delilah back with a single phone call and a car ride. I spoke with James for the first time one-on-one by impulsively running across the city. Helena waved away any fears I had of her hating me.

Life is hard, no doubt about that, but not everything has to be hard. Some things are easier than you think, and I wish I had learned this a long time ago.

Brother,

Somedays I feel these compulsions.

These urges that I feel as if the only thing preventing me from doing it is the softness of the couch, the waiting customers, the drone of upcoming tests and final assignments.

Thoughts race through my mind without my own creation and I cannot help but wonder why. I am defensive and want to keep this, but I feel like I must, like it is almost time, but I do not know why or what.

For so long, I could not look at my reflection and see the ghost staring back at me. I turned away when I used the microwave. I kept my eyes down on the bus. I broke the bathroom mirror with cut knuckles and Maamaa cried.

I finally let them put up the new mirror and I marvel at this new person.

She feels wrong but I know she is me.

She feels wrong because she is only me.

Wisps of black escaping the band are longer than your hair ever was. Eyes bright and faraway, still no sign of a pupil. I look in my new mirror and see only me.

There always was only me.

I was not meant to be your mirror in the same way you were not meant to be mine.

We were not reflections, we were similar. We were not the same, we were contrasted in ways unseen.

I see the difference in the mirror and yet I feel the need for more.

I have taken to huddling in the library and the *Apitiwin* room, in a safe place meant for students who look like me but also welcome to those who don't. I read the books and the authors instead of my study notes. I have a thirst for knowledge in the only way I feel capable of. I am scared to properly ask with *asemaa* in hand.

It is no surprise we felt this way.

It is a change in our genetic code, a possible change in brain chemistry from events centuries, decades, years ago. No matter the efforts MaamaaBaabaa put in, it was bound to happen, and we were not prepared for it.

We clung to each other for support but took it too far.

We were doomed from the start, and you will never have the opportunity to explore what this means, what our relationship to the land and cosmos means. But I do.

If not now, then when. If not then, then now. Why not now? There is so much space in a lifetime and I possess the blessing to spend it discovering where I fit in this world.

I did it, Brother,

On a whim I closed my eyes and reached forward, knowledge of the general direction but no idea of the colors. A quick sketch facing away, the night turning into day, and I find I have made a picture.

My first creation since I walked that rubber mat alone.

It is a mess in the background, but I can envision what to put in the foreground. We grew up on stories and I believe I can tell them with my colors.

We always shared everything.

A room, friends, parents, clothing, a job, our appearance.

Nothing belonged to only one of us. Except for brushes and pens. You had your writing and secret scribblings. I had my paints.

Now all that is left of you are the remaining fragments of your last year but there is plenty left of me. I never wrote before if it did not include a deadline, aside from that one time your pestering got to me.

However, I felt that same urge to pick up any writing utensil and paper at the end of last winter. I began to address letters with no intention of them ever reaching their intended person. I began to write to you to try and make sense of a world that does not have you in it anymore. I handwrote letters with no destination and they have become a journal.

This has become a shared experience of something new, but I do not think I will do it forever.

Taking up unsent letters and addressed journal entries has been a pleasant experience.

I know now that I can do both of the things our parents had wanted the individuals to do. I can write and paint. I do not need to align myself with one narrative, with one hobby. There is so much at my fingertips, and it feels overwhelming, but it also feels calming.

It is calming because I know that if I want to try something new or reinvent myself completely one day, I know that I can. The resources are out there, and I can do anything.

The knowledge that I can do anything if I just take the patience to try it feels like a high. I still haven't tried drugs and absolutely refuse to because of your end but life is starting to feel like my own personal pill.

Brother,

I feel as if I am beginning to breathe again. My heart beats on its own and my lungs accept oxygen for most of the day.

Things are getting better, but they will never be the same. I am working on accepting that now. I can let my mind wonder and wish but I must adapt to my new life.

A life that is solely mine.

I have a lot of my own things now. Delilah has been coming over whenever possible to help me sort and listen to me yammer on about the past and you and the memories I once held hidden between my ribs. She listens and asks questions at appropriate times and aids in choosing what to keep and what to get rid of.

The room looks empty now, but I have plans for how to fill in the gaps.

For so long I spent my life trying to be you and reflecting you. I never thought to be my own person. Being whole, being your own person, is a skill everyone must acquire in order to feel at peace in the world.

I am working on it.

I am trying awfully hard.

I do this game with myself where I see myself from other's eyes. I see the girl that once looked like someone else. Strip away the appearance and what is left? A person. Someone worth existing with the living. I deserve to choose life. I deserve to create my own life and my own identity.

I was never a half and should not have allowed myself to be treated as such. I am my own person, I am whole.

We didn't deserve the tangling of lifelines; all it did was choke us.

Something I long for the most is one last conversation with you.

A moment in time to tell you that I felt the same aches you did. The same emptiness. We were so similar and so ready to ignore individuality that it was our undoing.

I am the last one standing and I do not think that what I felt when you left was an absence of you. I think it was an absence of myself. No longer could I fill the emptiness with our adjoining identities, I was instead left with this empty outline of a person waiting to be created, to be discovered.

After my last exam, I walked in the cold to the building that has quickly begun to feel like another home. I have a list of books that I wanted to read before the semester ended but I ran out of time because I needed to study.

So instead of waiting for next semester, I took them. I don't know if I was allowed to do that, but they will get them back in the new year.

I read the books aloud like I used to read aloud to you. It makes me feel like I am telling your spirit the things we could have learnt together. The books we should have read together to keep our promise to MaamaaBaabaa.

The walls still close in some days. I am an outline trying to fill myself with only myself, but it is so lonely. I did not know what loneliness felt like before this year.

For the first time in my life, I am alone.

You are not here, and you never will be again, but that doesn't mean we are not together. In my dreams you got better, and we were able to take this journey together.

Instead, I must do this alone, and I will have to become accustomed to living life this way. There are so many things we should have done together that I now must do alone. Stealing books on our culture (with the honest intention of returning them) just happens to be one of them.

Being alone isn't the worst thing in the world, it just feels like it in the moment where the silence is so deafening that I want to scream to fill the void. Out of the many hurdles I know life will throw at me, accepting loneliness is a priority.

Amazingly, they gave me permission.

I would stand in front of the paint display for what felt like hours trying to decide on a singular color to paint my room until it became so overwhelming I almost felt like giving up.

Last week James had given me the idea to paint my walls like a canvas. The way I used to when we were little. I've never done a proper mural before, and my room sounds like a good place to start.

I do not know what I will paint yet, but a thick layer of primer and plain white is a necessary start. I can always do it in sections, weaving the story of the shared life that existed onto the bare walls. Not everything has to be completed immediately, and sometimes, it is okay to completely start over if you are not satisfied.

I told Baabaa I want to dedicate a bookshelf in the store to Indigenous works. I have a stack on the bedside table that I am reading. I don't know another way to find the culture on my own, but reading is never a bad idea. A lot of the books are memoirs, and their lives aren't so different from the ones we have in our little family. Abuse, foster systems, substance abuse, etc.

We were never alone in surviving a country that spends centuries trying to erase us; so many others have gone through the same and more. A few of them are still in the process of finding themselves like I am.

I will return the books when I am done with them, but Baabaa agrees that it is important to keep written works such as these in stock. (I saw him reading the one book I had already finished.)

My semester break will be spent searching for new inventory that we want the shop to carry in the new year. He even said that although we are a secondhand bookstore, it wouldn't be the end of the world if we bought directly from the authors to read and sell their works.

It feels like there is so much more to say and do.

These letters to you should have been recounts of our adventures together and a more accurate expression of my grieving but instead they had simply become an outlet. I took the year off from my art journals and began creating a letter diary of sorts. These letters have become my tether to the real world, the only thing bringing me back out of my mind to where our memories are home.

Going over them, I can see a vague timeline of my grief and my new life that is still under construction. Even though I am running out of paper, my life must continue.

We did the last-minute shopping before the stores became busy with the last-minute holiday shoppers. I have my new paint cans and brushes. Baabaa found a gift for Maamaa and kept pestering me about what I want for my birthday. I almost said you but managed to stop myself. Tomorrow it will be officially one year since your passing, and I will turn eighteen, an age you never achieved.

You may not have graduated high school or reached the "legal" age, but I have, and I will. You did things I never want to, and I will do the things you never got to.

My next step involves my birthday request. The only scissors we have in the building come from an office supply store or a knife block set. We have never had our hair cut and were taught to care for it as soon as we could sit still for a few minutes.

A few of the books have said it was a way to move on from the past and start anew. Mainly for grief and recovery. This is exactly what I need to officially start this new chapter of my life.

I like to think you're watching over me. If I could, I would add art to my letters for you, but I don't think "watching over" works exactly like that.

Instead, I sit on the rooftop of our building in the middle of winter and read my letters to the wind in hopes of reaching you.

Sometimes it feels like the wind is answering back but that may just be the new sensation of exposed flesh on my neck.

Anyway, I hope you've found the peace you were looking for. I am beginning to find mine.

Acknowledgements

I want to start by thanking my husband, Chase, who believed in me and my writing even when I did not. Who held me when the writing started to hit a little too close to home. A heartfelt thank you to my best friends, Daniela and Treonna, for being my first proofreaders before I would let anyone else read my story. I couldn't have finished if it weren't for your continuous encouragement. Nimamowendam to my cuzzins who read this before the publishing companies did. Even when it got too hard to read, you continued to believe in my writing skills.

Thanks to everyone at DCB Young Readers, without you this book would not exist. A special thanks to Barry Jowett, my amazing editor. You are the person who made me believe in not just being a writer, but an *author*.

PHOTO CREDIT: KIERAN JOSHUA DAVIS

Mackenzie Angeconeb (Aan-ji-qui-ni-ai'ib) (she/they) is an Anishinaabekwe author and educator from Lac Seul First Nation. She began writing while attending university, incorporating themes from the common pains of Indigenous youths and families, as well as her own coming-of-age. In their spare time, they like to paint with watercolours and acrylics, bead earrings, read second-hand books, or learn Anishinaabemowin when their schedule permits. *The Fragments that Remain* is her debut novel. Angeconeb lives in Sioux Lookout, ON.

We acknowledge the sacred land on which Cormorant Books operates. It has been a site of human activity for 15,000 years. This land is the territory of the Huron-Wendat and Petun First Nations, the Seneca, and most recently, the Mississaugas of the Credit River. The territory was the subject of the Dish With One Spoon Wampum Belt Covenant, an agreement between the Iroquois Confederacy and Confederacy of the Ojibway and allied nations to peaceably share and steward the resources around the Great Lakes. Today, the meeting place of Toronto is still home to many Indigenous people from across Turtle Island. We are grateful to have the opportunity to work in the community, on this territory.

We are also mindful of broken covenants and the need to strive to make right with all our relations.